UNSEE

Military Sexual Trauma Memoir

AUTHOR

VANESSA MORBECK

ISBN:

DEDICATION

I dedicate this book to my consistent growth and perseverance to not pass my generational trauma on to my daughter. This book originally was a memoir to my daughter after my experience which took my life and granted me another. I also dedicate this book to all those who have, are currently, or no longer with us due to their sacrifices in the United States Military and those affected by MST.

Lastly, I want to dedicate this book to the ever-evolving soul named -
Jay Bum Park. (Yes, The Korean American Musician)
Read below to find out why.

I dedicate this book on behalf of my late Grandfather, PFC Ronald A. MORBECK who passed this year October 17, 2023, and his son PFC, Robert F. MORBECK, my deceased father.

CONTENTS

Content warning: This book includes the topics of sexual assault, suicide, and rape.
If you or someone you know is in crisis, call or text the National Suicide Prevention Lifeline at 988. The hotline is staffed 24/7 by trained counselors who can offer free, confidential support. Spanish speakers can call 1-888-628-9454. People who are deaf or hard of hearing can call 1-800-799-4889.

ACKNOWLEDGMENTS

Normally this is for acknowledgment, but I want to use this space to express my thanks and gratitude for life. For those that take the time to read this Resource Guide thank you. If I can inspire and inform, or essentially save one life then I thank the Universe for allowing me to have a second chance at life. I am writing this book for others to get to know my story and to be able to give a voice to the many incidents the public does not know about when it comes to personal trauma in the Military. I had to sustain 15 cases of sexual violence ranging from wrongful sexual contact, nine sexual assaults, one sodomy, one retaliation and reprisal, rape, one indecent exposure and one abusive sexual contact. Then face the backlash of reporting in terms of retaliation and forced into medical retirement.

1 INTRODUCTION

I was born in Nuremburg, Germany on a Military base as an American citizen. I was born prematurely at 2 lbs. and 0 ounces. I grew up in Milwaukee, Wisconsin. My childhood experiences are the least but happy. I grew up to an alcoholic mother with severe mental illness, but as I grow older, I forgave her. That is where my trauma started. I learned that I was not important enough or that my needs did not matter. I learned to walk on eggshells every day and that at the age of 8 I needed to be the mother of the family. My mother left at a young age. I was the oldest living in the home.

I came from an internal family of molestation from my cousin, abuse from my mother, and misery. My stepfather is great to me, he and his mom are my biggest supporters. My stepfather has been in Law Enforcement for over 20 years and is also an Army veteran. One of my other siblings is also a Law Enforcement Officer. However, I am the first Federal Law Enforcement Officer, first female veteran in my family.

I have six siblings. One younger brother and five sisters. I am the third eldest but second in line since my eldest sister passed away when she was 18 months old with my father (PFC,19 years old) in a vehicle collision in Germany.

But my real intense trauma did not start until I was in the United States Army.

Now that you know my demographics. By heritage I am Hispanic, Swedish, German and I went to college and received an associate degree. I went from being bullied in school, to being the outcast in high school. I later got tired of my mother, when she was around, dragging me by the hair, the constant arguments, being in fear of going home, dragging me down the steps, throwing me across the floor, the constant abuse that taught me I did not matter.

These short stories are compiled case by case, so the story is outspoken, genuine, and raw. Little did I know I and other servicemembers would have had to suffer sexual abuse in the Military. So that is where the story begins. These are all true events, the only thing that is changed is the assailant's names and any other name that does not need to be disclosed for HIPPA reasons.

It wouldn't be right to write a book and not tell the whole story for I thought of omitting some chapters due to irrelevance. Today I will be brave enough to share the whole story from my life experiences point of view.

Vanessa Morbeck hugs her daughter, Ariana Johnston, 8, inside her kitchen at her apartment at the Veterans Village in the Frankford section of Philadelphia.
Heather Khalifa / Staff Photographer

2 "ZERO TOLERANCE"

The original title for this was for a college class I was in, and this is the article I written July 13, 2014.

Imagine: On New Year's Eve of century at 8 years old is when the I was molested by my female cousin which influenced my sexual orientation for years to come. Even though many years have passed since the beginning of my assaults, 12 years to be exact, the two most terrifying incidents are the ones I endured in South Korea during my first tour (deployment) in the United States Army.

Consider now this excerpt that I am about to share, while as I reread; Tears start to form in my eyes: "As he kissed me on the lips, I didn't kiss back." She stated, "He continued to kiss my breasts from left to right, simultaneously, and started tracing his lips down my stomach while placing his hand in my pants." She stated: As I kept tightening my legs, he kept asking "No?", but when he couldn't get me to stop tightening my legs, he proceeded to start kissing me and playing with my chest the same way as before...As he decided to forcefully try and pry my legs open, eventually I became numb and couldn't resist anymore."

As I begin to type this, I am clenching my fist at the same time. The Army's main program is called S.H.A.R.P, which is abbreviated for Sexual Harassment/Assault Response and Prevention (SHARP Website ref 8), alongside the Criminal Investigation Command and rushing to the Emergency Room to receive a S.A.N.E Kit (Sexual Assault Nurse Examiners). More importantly, even though this situation is viewed as being negative, the fact that I am still alive, breathing, and trying to succeed is good enough for me to continue being who I am. The Uniformed Code of Military Justice defines sexual assault as "any person subject to this chapter who – Commits a sexual act upon another person by – threatening or placing that other person in fear; causing bodily harm, Quid Pro Quo, impairing by drugs or intoxication... so forth." (Manual for Court-Martial United States 352).

While Army Regulation 600-20 Army Command Policy defines Sexual Assault as: Sexual assault is a crime defined as intentional sexual contact, characterized by use of force, physical threat, or abuse of authority or when the victim does not or cannot consent..."Consent" will not be deemed or construed to mean the failure by the victim to offer physical resistance. Consent is not given when a person uses force, threat of force, or coercion or when the victim is asleep, incapacitated, or unconscious. (Chapter8-4)

In my case, even though all these facts were present both times, they were still deemed "Unfounded". What does that mean? While researching many articles, the word "Unfounded" populated several pertaining to false reports and the lack of evidence thereof. Unfounded does not mean that the event never occurred, it just means there is not enough physical evidence or probable cause that the incident can be legally prosecuted in the court of law.

Consider now, if you were put in a situation where such an offense occurred, only four months later authorities tell you that there is not enough evidence to prosecute this person therefore the case is "Unfounded". The first time I heard that word was during my first assault in South Korea, the facts do not matter, it was the outcome and events thereafter that affected me and still affect me the most.

On the night of the assault, December 1st, 2012, my supervisor rushed me to the Emergency Room for nurse to evaluate me and begin.

The process of "reporting". I would advise all service members to start with a restricted report, you can always go unrestricted later. There are only three personnel you can talk about a sexual incident: **A medical staff, law enforcement or SHARP representative.** This is particularly important. If you tell anyone else like your supervisor, they are not sworn to protect your confidentiality and it will compromise your restricted reporting and make your report "Unrestricted".

This is where the victimization came in to play and it was here that I was forever stigmatized with a label above my head that told the world I was a survivor of sexual violence. Reporting a sexual assault and harassment case is very humiliating.

Now imagine, you are in a room with your supervisor and the medical provider sitting there in tears, scared, and humiliated. The provider asks you to tell him what happened, the sexual acts, and jotting "he said, she said" right in front of you. Nonetheless, during the process they collect what is called a "Rape Kit" where the use.

of black lights, cotton swabs, inspections of bruises, all evidence they can collect, clothing articles, with hair and saliva collections. When all is said and done, at least in my case, I had to spend three to four days in a room with investigators and no sleep, no food, and held against my will to leave. Have you ever been interrogated? I felt ashamed, humiliated, embarrassed, and like I was a criminal.

You know it is funny, because if one person looked at me, no one would believe that I have endured so much agony. Most people view me as being this genuine, positive, outgoing person who probably grew up in a white picket fence house with love and appreciation from having a good childhood. Intermittently, there are other procedures in the process, but I want to convey how I felt after the incidents. After reporting to Criminal Investigation Command, my story was out, all the Sharp Representatives could say was, "Good job!" and "That was the right thing to do, you spoke up!" but deep down inside I felt disgusted with myself, how I could let this happen to me again. These feelings were deeper than when I was a child, when the assaults occurred my body went numb, and my mind was barely involved. There are three things that evoke the ***flight, fight, or freeze*** response in your body when you undergo a traumatic event.

My body felt it was in danger enough to evoke the freeze response for most of these assaults for these offenders to not kill me if I resisted and threats were made to harm me further if I resisted. That was the beginning of being victimized, and it just got worse throughout the year. Immediately after reporting, I had to return to the barracks only to find out my Commander wanted to speak with me, hence I walked to her office only to be humiliated once again.

I was voluntold to sleep on a cot in the staff duty office and monitored for the first three days after the assault as a suicide risk, from there I was allowed back in my room and only allowed to leave the Battalion if I had one of my NCO's (Supervisors) presents. During that treatment which lasted well over a month, I was forced to attend behavioral health classes, all the while being threatened by my Commander to be chaptered due to her interpretation of my "failure to adapt to the Military environment". Furthermore, I was out casted by my unit because a corrupt little bird told everyone I was assaulted. Please consider the possibility, by understanding and imagining yourself in my boots, that by being isolated and mistreated, any Soldier would want to take their own life. I finally understood why the

The military has so many suicides, and in those conditions, all I could do was huddle on the floor wailing out loud, crying through the walls, and screaming at myself. The feeling of disgust grew deeper and deeper until one day I looked in the mirror and decided to volunteer for the base in MWR (Morale Welfare and Recreation) program.

After that uplifting event, I was able to move forward and I attempted to train for the Air Assault Mobile unit that was coming to Camp Casey, South Korea. As the negative stigma followed me throughout my 1-year tour I reluctantly treaded lightly up until I was assaulted YET again at the end of my tour. I wish I never had reported this second time due to the first being so traumatic and the investigators "victim shaming/blaming" and continuously asking me or warning me of making a false statement.

Unfortunately, this second assault ended up following me to my current unit which I am still being in a sense, victimized for. Remarkably, I was able to pass all the rigors of the Air Assault entry test. The entry test consisted of an obstacle course, rope climbing, and a 12-mile ruck with full gear and a cap time of 3 hours to pre-qualify. I passed it in the dead freezing cold, with full gear and weapon, assault pack and helmet within 2 hours and 50 minutes. I was the only female in my battalion S1 to try out for this Air Assault prequalification. In my mind I thought, "I can do this, I am not going to allow these assaults to overcome me, and I will prove my ability to continue the fight."

As I have demonstrated the power of being resilient and persevering, I would never have made it to this point where I am today. If I did not have the courage and willpower to overcome fear of reprisal, disrespect among my past units, and myself deprecation. I speak to you not as an advocate but as a survivor of sexual violence. Seventy-five percent of my life has been disastrous and traumatic so far. The other twenty-five are content and beautiful. The strength that I have now counters the amount of pain that I endured, and currently I am happy and healthy in life, and I have a few people to thank for that. I would love in this life or the next to help others, especially survivors of sexual violence in this aspect. Women and men should not just feel but BE empowered by their strength to overcome all barriers. The more people I get this message to, the more the world may understand the seriousness of this, and maybe, just maybe someday... there will be zero tolerance in everyone's mind.

3 WHAT IS MST?

What is MST (Military Sexual Trauma)?

The VA (Veteran Affairs) uses the term “military sexual trauma” (MST) to refer to sexual assault or threatening sexual harassment experienced during military service. MST includes any sexual activity during military service in which you are involved against your will or when unable to say no.

Examples include:

- Being pressured or coerced into sexual activities, such as with threats of negative treatment if you refuse to cooperate or with promises of better treatment.
- Sexual contact or activities without your consent, including when you were asleep or intoxicated.
- Being overpowered or physically forced to have sex.
- Being touched or grabbed in a sexual way that made you uncomfortable, including during “hazing” experiences.
- Comments about your body or sexual activities that you found threatening.
- Unwanted sexual advances that you found threatening.

Some of the difficulties both female and male survivors of **MST** (military sexual trauma) may include but not all inclusive:

Strong emotions: feeling; having intense, sudden emotional responses to things; feeling all the time.
Feelings of numbness: feeling emotionally "flat"; trouble feeling love or happiness.

Trouble sleeping bad dreams or Trouble with attention, and memory: trouble staying focused; often finding your mind wandering; having a hard time remembering things drinking to excess or using drugs daily; getting drunk or "high" to cope with memories or unpleasant feelings; drinking to fall asleep.

Trouble with reminders of the sexual trauma: or "jumpy" all the time; not feeling safe; going out of your way to avoid reminders of the trauma; trouble trusting others feeling alone or not connected to others; abusive relationships; or authority figures Physical health problems: sexual issues; weight or eating problems; stomach or bowel problems.

Possible Effects of Sexual Violence:

Self-Harm- Deliberate self-harm, or self-injury, is when a person inflicts physical harm on himself or herself, usually in secret.

Sexually Transmitted Infections- A sexually transmitted infection (STI) is a bacterial or viral infection passed from one person to another through vaginal, anal, or oral contact.

Substance Abuse - If you are concerned that you are using substances in a way that could be harmful to your health or have concerns for someone you care about, consider learning more about the warning signs and places to find support.

Dissociation- is one of the many defense mechanisms the brain can use to cope with the trauma of sexual violence.

Panic Attacks - A panic attack is a sudden feeling of intense fear and anxiety that happens in situations when there may be no immediate danger. They tend to affect people who have experienced trauma, abuse, or high levels of stress.

Eating Disorders and Self-image - Sexual violence can affect survivors in many ways, including perceptions of the body and feelings of control.

Pregnancy - If you were recently raped, you may have concerns about becoming pregnant from the attack.

Sleep Disorders - Symptoms of sleep disorders can include trouble falling or staying asleep, sleeping at unusual times of day, or sleeping for longer or shorter than usual.

Suicide and Suicide Attempts - Suicide is preventable and suicidal thoughts are not permanent. If you are thinking about suicide, there are resources to give you the support you need to get through this tough time. Call **1 (800) 273-8255** (Also a song by Logic) and Press 1 to be connected VA CRISIS LINE.

Post-Traumatic Stress Disorder

(PTSD), including flashbacks, nightmares, severe anxiety, and uncontrollable thoughts. **Depression,** including prolonged sadness, feelings of hopelessness, unexplained crying, weight loss or gain, loss of energy or interest in activities previously enjoyed.

Impact

People of all genders, ages, sexual orientations, racial and ethnic backgrounds, and branches of service have experienced MST. Like other types of traumas, MST can negatively affect a person's mental and physical health, even many years later. Things you may experience could include:

- Disturbing memories or nightmares
- Difficulty feeling safe.
- Feelings of depression or numbness
- Using alcohol or other drugs to numb or escape from negative feelings.
- Feeling isolated from other people
- Difficulties with anger, irritability, or other strong emotions
- Self-doubt, self-blame, or decreased self-esteem.

- Issues with sleep
- Physical health problems

If you are having any current difficulties related to MST, VA is here to support you in whatever way will help you best — from learning more about how MST affects people, to treatment that helps you cope with how MST is impacting your life currently, or if you prefer, treatment that involves discussing your experiences in more depth.

For questions about treatment and health care options related to MST, talk with an MST Coordinator at a VA health care facility near you.

Now that you are familiar with the terms and symptoms it will be easier to follow along with the incidents. Below is the harrowing and somewhat explicit real-life cases of what happened to me which molded me to who I am today. Although many people like to say the mantra, "What doesn't kill you makes you stronger" or "Those situations happened to you, but they don't have to define you". One going through it might not believe you until they learn to accept and process that trauma. Because for us, for a short or long period of time it indeed did define or engulf us. Like reliving a waking nightmare in the daily flesh engulfed by memories we can't suppress until the duress is too much to bear, a living hell a nightmare ensnares. But nonetheless we can prevail and overcome day by day with the right resources and seeking the ability to want to self-improve.

4 REAL WONZ

The next following Chapters entail most of the compilation of all my assault reports verbatim from the police reports I made with the Criminal Investigation Command or in civilian terms Investigation Unit. This text is placed here as a trigger warning. The Topics we will discuss may be triggering for some or uncomfortable to read and visualize. DO NOT PROCEED FORWARD IF TRIGGERED, you can always skip chapters.

The Navy Recruiter

Who: Chinese (American) Navy Recruiter who spoke Cantonese

What: Sexual Assault

When: September 20, 2011

Where: San Gabriel Navy Recruiting Station, California

Age: 19

How:

I met him at a store near Starbucks and a Vietnamese Bahn Mi restaurant he was in his tan Navy mess uniform with sunglasses on in a beret. I wore a USC shirt and sweat Capri maroon in color w/ USC etched in gold font. It was a Tuesday and sunny. It was in the afternoon and evening by the time I arrived home. I was 19 years of age. I am not sure what his height or age was. Approximately 28- 35 years old. He arrived with a portable laptop in a bag and set it on the table. I remember making physical contact by greeting and shaking his hand. He never took his sunglasses off until we got in the car. I sat there taking the pre-asvab. An hour passed and I noticed him staring in my general direction the whole time and leaning over me to help me when I got stuck. Once we finished, he told me to come with him to go back to the recruiting station for height and weight.

He met me in my city Alhambra, CA. I got in his car, passenger side and asked him questions about the Navy, himself, his age, languages he spoke and told him he was handsome. Once we parked and pulled up to the recruiting station, he unlocked the door, and we went inside.

The building lights were off. He turned them on, walked to the desk, and shuffled some papers around. I walked in a few steps and saw a wall with navy recruits looked at it, and asked a question, and walked further into the station toward the back of the door. Before I proceeded, he showed me a picture on his phone and told me had a child. I did not notice he had a ring on his finger.

I continued to walk to the back of the office, my back facing the door. Unexpectedly, he pulls my ponytail back and I collapse on to him from behind, his arms wrap around me and on to my breast, he squeezes them. My face blushes and he pull my hand and pulls me into the small storage room next to the entrance. He was against the wall next to the door unzips his pants and belt and pulls his penis out, telling me to "*suck it*" and asks me " *If I ever had an Asian cock inside my mouth*". I placed my mouth on his male appendage as ordered while he puts his hand on the back of my head and neck thrusting it pulling my hair while he thrusts his male appendage in and out of my mouth. My eyes began to tear while I was on my knees and I yelled "No" out while his male appendage was in my mouth. After that he just stopped and told me "*Let's go*".

He pulls his male appendage back in and zips up his pants then takes me back home.

On the car ride home, he told me "*Not to say anything*", "*Delete it from my mind*", "*It never happened.*" He then called me after I got home, and I answered. My boyfriend was there so I just acknowledged. In that moment I was nervous, and I ended up telling my boyfriend happened, but I was ignored. I went to my scheduled college classes as normal the next day and decided to tell my college professor what happened. The heavily influenced me to report it.

The San Gabriel Police Department has records on file for this incident.

I went to the police station a few days later and they wanted to do a wiretap, but by the time we got to the recruiting station the Navy had got wind of it and moved him to another unit. I later found out in the investigation that he "stonewalled" them or remained silent and did not cooperate in the investigation.

I was at **MEPS (**Military Entrance Processing center) that month signing my Initial Entry Paperwork for the United States Army.

This case was unfounded not because it never happened but due to the negligence of the assailants' lack testimony.

Basic Training

Who: Private Linehan* Caucasian Male Basic Receptee, A Company,
1-34th Infantry

What: Sexual Assault

When: May 15th, 2012 (Started April 4, 2012, Graduated June 14, 2012)

Where: Live Night Fire Exercise, Fort Jackson, South Carolina

Me: Female, 20 Yrs. Old, Uniform ACU's (Army Combat Uniform) with weapon

On May 15th, 2012, between the hours of 2000 (8 PM) to 2100(9 PM) my platoon was supposed to do the NIC (night infiltration course) here at Fort Jackson "Victory Hammer", but it began to pour rain with lighting involved. When lighting is involved, the Soldiers must sit under an LPA (lighting protection area) which at the time was dark with dimmed red lights, but they were so faint the area had no light at all, loud from rain hitting the ground, crowded and tightly compacted with Soldiers.

I was one of them. I remember being in the third row, toward the center of the LPA ground but more toward the right. As I sat there leaned back-to-back against my battle buddy, who kept complaining ever so often about me shifting, knowing that I was trying to get away from Private Line. As I was just sitting there on the ground with my head resting against my knees Line begins to run his left hand up my lower leg then traces it to my thigh after a few minutes or so, he then continues to up to my crotch and begin to rub at the upper mid area for several minutes, by then I am still trying to move away slightly scooching back after each attempt.

Dead tired and scared but never having dealt with these situations before, I just let him get it over with and move on. However, at the very moment I remember being so tired that I kept dozing in and out, drifting from sleep to awake just letting it happen as I occasionally tried to move but my battle buddy kept complaining. I figured, me trying to move would tell him to stop, at times I even placed my hand there pushing it away. even when he tried to move his hand down my pants, as much of this event took place on top of my clothes. He still would not stop. Dozing in and out I noticed his face looking at me as he kept doing it while nodding at me, but I gave him no response except trying to move while returning to rest my head on my knees once more. At no time did I give him any consent, nor did I appreciate that gesture.

This case was my first case that was FOUNDED, the assailant received Article 15 and graduated then went to Advance Individual Training and remained in the Army.

These are evidence photos from the investigations from US ARMY CID. Fort Jackson, SC (2012)

These are evidence photos from the investigations from US ARMY CID. Camp Casey, South Korea (2012)

Basic Training Bullying

It took me a few days to report because I was being discriminated/harassed by my female peers for their assumption of my sexual orientation and Drill Sergeant (DS) Rogers.

When I did muster enough courage to report the mistreatment and sexual assault to DS Rogers and DS Aurora. Oh, man was that an issue.

DS Rogers ordered me to refrain from being in the female bay latrine (bathroom)f at the same time the other females were bathing. I was isolated. I was either the first to shower or the last, mostly last. I could not even go to the latrine to pee, shower, or clean. I was ordered to do everything alone, by myself. This persisted for a few weeks. This is a form of social retaliation with threats coming from a few female recruits, "to beat my ass and to hurt me". As a result, in reporting both the female's mistreatment, the DS's Action and my sexual assault incident I was threatened with disciplinary action if what "I" was doing continued. I stood at attention, practically begging, to the company Commander that they (the female recruits) were lying and expressed how I was being treated by the DS.

As a result, Private Line and I lost our family day as unfavorable action. My experiences in basic training surrounding these events affected me by "shutting down" any evidence of me being a lesbian later bisexual, further at my new duty stations. I was being “silenced". By the time I graduated basic training most of the lesbian and gay Soldiers dropped out, except one other and me being bisexual at that time. That was pivotal year because the ruling over the government allowed LGBTQ plus persons’ to be openly their selves.

Advanced Individual Training – School

Charlie Company 369th Adjutant General Battalion Fort Jackson, South Carolina 29207-5200

AIT – June 14, 2012, to August 15, 2012

By the time we advanced to AIT still dealing with the mistreatment, harassment, and continuous threats to harm me from Private Panini. She was the Alpha in our sleeping quarters. Panini, her girlfriend, and some of the same females in Basic were still spreading rumors, teasing me, and taking advantage of me. Panini's daily threats to "kick my ass" struck fear in me and caused me to further "silence and shut down". I reported this to Sergeant First Class Jonas, he handled it a few times, but she persisted. While in AIT, Panini and I had to pull CQ, patrolling the hallways, cleaning and I attempted to use that chance to reconcile our differences. To no avail, she used that opportunity to learn about my life and take that information and spread it like wildfire, some of our conflicts had her literally at my throat, jumping out at me, made violent gestures to jump at me physically. Her girlfriend had to pull her off from attempting to harm me.

Eventually be both permanently changed stations to South Korea, where I saw Panini a few months after getting there and learned she was doing everything she could to get out of service. She ended up leaving the Army before I arrived at Joint-Base Lewis McChord. There were two or three times both I and Panini ended up in SFC Jonas office because of reporting her actions.

On the night of our pass, I do not remember the incident, but my friend remembers some excruciating evidence about how Private Himura and his friends were gloating about running a train on me.

I was convinced drugged, and they recorded two videos, me in the barracks in the shower and of the sexual assault. I do not remember drinking, but I do remember alcohol being present. My colleague agreed to write up a testimony on her observations of my treatment in Basic, AIT, and that incident. My perpetrators were spreading rumors that I was a "lying cunt, cum bucket, that I liked it" after passing around those videos to the unit. I was called a "whore" and out casted by my peers.

This case was **unfounded**, predominantly due to the statute of limitations, lack of evidence and me being unaware of it.

Authors thoughts: This may or not be a popular opinion, I never knew what sexual assault experiences until I joined the U.S. Army.

At this point regardless of gender if this happened to you would you have chosen to get out of the military or stay?

5 CAMP, CASEY SOUTH KOREA

Republic of Korea was my first duty station and I worked/lived there for approximately a year from September 2012 to 2013. I was assigned to 70th Brigade Support Battalion on Camp Casey, APO AE in the city of **Dongducheon** which is 8 miles from the border of the two Koreas. Within a one-year time span I experienced several types of military sexual trauma from Korean and American Soldiers. I lived on this base for one year with all five assailants. My unit at the time refused to allow me to leave the country on what the U.S. Army calls a "compassionate reassignment" due to incidents such as read below. I survived five incidents. Out of all the places and times I was sexually assaulted South Korea had the most impact both negative light and a positive one.

Camp Casey, South Korea Part one

On Sunday December 1, 2012, around 1200 hours, I met a Korean Soldier named Katusa Ji and walked off the military post to take a taxi right outside Jihaeng. From Jihaeng, we got off at the main plaza around where Dunkin Donuts is. From there we walked a few doors down to a Korean barbeque restaurant, ate chow from 1300 to 1400 then around 1430 went to get some coffee at Dunkin Donuts.

This took place like a Korean karaoke bar. I suggested going to a real movie theater in Uijeongbu, but he insisted on that being too far and wanted to go straight to Marty's Cafe. Once we arrived at Marty's Cafe, we exchanged slippers, locked up our shoes for about 1500 then proceeded to the room with the pink futon like set with large pink pillows. At the time I felt extremely uncomfortable, "*like this doesn't feel right*". My intuition was begging me to leave, if only I listened.

I asked the Korean Soldier Katusa if this room was used for more than watching movies and he said "*No, don't worry about it*". We decided to watch an American war movie called "Act of Valor"; the time was set for about two hours. Ten minutes into the movie he started to hug me from behind and grope my breast and asked, "Are these natural?". I did not give a response. He then proceeded to touch them, a few moments later he told me he was hesitant to place his hand inside my bra because his hands were cold.

Then he proceeded, as I was squirming trying to just pay attention to the movie. He then kissed my neck, despite. I just continued to squirm because I felt uncomfortable and unsafe. Soon after I was pulled on to my back and he went in between my legs. I crawled on my back to move away from him, but he just persisted, moving closer and closer until he was in between my legs again. He pulled my dress up until my bra was exposed. Once the bra was exposed, he pulled my left breast out and started sucking on it lightly than harder, then licked my neck and that continued for what seemed like minutes.

He then placed his left hand down the slit of my shorts, I would pull his hand away, but he kept persisting. I resisted a few times, once he finally got to the point of placing his hand within my shorts, he then went deeper in to massaging my genital area. I continued to pull his hand away, but as he became hornier, he then proceeded to stick his fingers into me, While I was defending myself, I decided to continue to watch the movie for as long as I could withstand.

Eventually he got my clothes and tried to stick his male appendage inside of me, but I wrapped my legs around him and contracted them outward to push him back so he could not penetrate me. He continued to persist. After several attempts and me giving up because of his strength, I just let him finish. Alongside the attempts he continued to squeeze, lick, and fondle my breasts. He then kissed down my stomach and tried to orally lick me, but as he got to the bridge of my stomach, I told him, "No". During the time he was doing all of this, I kept saying "NO, I do not want this, I have not showered. No, please don't, I haven't showered".

I also told him I do not like unwanted sexual advances, nor do I like having any sexual relationships while in a relationship, which he knew, nor do I like having sex without showering. As I would say this phrase, he replied "He showered, and it is okay...!" He did not proceed with oral vaginal sex, but then kept continuously trying to penetrate me, as I kept evading by pushing him outward with my legs contracted. He continued to make more attempts to penetrate me, and that is when I looked at the timer. It said 01:24, meaning the time was ticking down.

I eventually gave in, so he pulled me up on him as if I was straddling him, tried to penetrate me in which he succeeded, but didn't quite make it, so he pushed me back down on to my back and penetrated me. It was about time for me to give up, admit that I lost, and just let him finish, as he penetrated me, he did it swift and hard, saying "He'd make it fast!" and he did. The next thing you know he is asking me if he can ejaculate inside. He ejaculated on my pelvic area.

This case was unfounded.

For your information: If you are ever stationed in South Korea. The Republic of Korea (ROKA) Army and South Korea does not prosecute sexual crimes like the United States Criminal Justice system, but this was in 2012 and 2013. Do your updated research.

These next few photos are my barracks room, the Korean Marty Café, and the totality of investigations during my career.

This is an image of "Marty's Café" taken from official investigation from the Army.

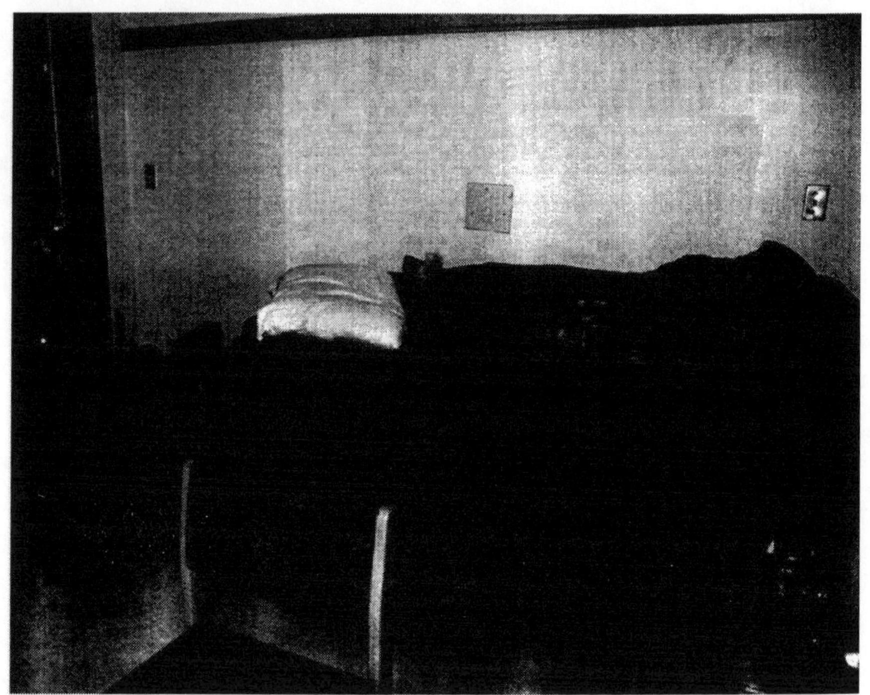

This is an image of my Barracks room 209 on Camp Casey, Dongducheon, South Korea taken from official investigation from the Army.

Air Assault School

Who: Caucasian Male
What: Sexual Assault
When: Winter 2013 – February 2013
Where: Camp Casey, South Korea (Gym on Casey Main)
Me: F, 21 years old, Workout Uniform
Rank: Private, E-2

How:

I knew him from Air Assault prequalification's exam; we pushed each other motivationally on the day of the 12-mile march. He was from a different unit than I was and enlisted. I ran to the gym a few days later. Before I left the gym, I ran in to him again. As I was about to leave, he brushed me up against the wall with his hand on the wall blocking me from escaping. I do not remember his age or name. He ordered me to give him oral sex and wanted to feel me up and asked, "When are we meeting again?" But by the time this incident occurred the gym was getting ready to close. I was frightened and called out to the Korean desk clerk and told him about it in Korean. The clerk drove me to my barracks across the street.

Staff Sergeant Mack

Who: Staff Sergeant Mack

What: Sexual Assault

When: Spring 2013 but prior to September 3rd, 2013, where: SASMO building, near the Tank Washer Rack, 70th BSB, Camp Casey, South Korea (Casey Main)

Rank: Private First Class, E-3

I was a Private First Class, E-3.

I do not remember the building number or his age. SFC Mack was the S6 NCOIC, while I was stationed in Camp Casey, South Korea. He appeared to be mixed African American; Light skinned, curly hair, B. eyes, Tall (approximately 6'2).

I remember it was night when SFC Mack invited four other lower ranking Soldiers to the building. We met up there because the Soldiers were throwing some type of party. It was me, SPC Carrot (Now a civilian.), PFC Crayons, SPC Oregano and another. I was the only female there. After eating pizza and drinking soda we all decided to watch a movie called "One Piece Film Z" Japanese Anime movie. We sat there watching it together all of us, and then out of nowhere the other Soldiers left. It was past midnight. I do not remember ever falling asleep that night by the time the assault was over it was morning time.

I was the only one left behind. He had told me to stay back because it was so late and that I could sleep there. I was not drinking alcohol.

He began kissing me while the movie was on. Then we started to get undressed. I cannot remember what I was wearing. I went along because I knew he was going to take it anyway; my body just freezes, and I became submissive.

He was of a higher rank than I by many.

He told me to get him wet and to "get him up". I did as I was told.

He had me sit there naked and told me to get on top after I got him off. While subsequently had me jack him off and give him head. I remember tasting the sweat in my mouth and the heat from his body, as before he pushed my head farther down on his male appendage repeatedly. He then had me get on top again until I got tired, then flipped me over and shoved his male appendage in missionary and then from behind. He penetrated me anally and vaginally. My body was exhausted, and I was pushing him to stop but he wanted to ejaculate inside of me. The projector of the movie was replaying the movie title screen because the movie was over hours before. He placed his mouth on my vagina to get it wet because I was not wet enough.

Remember the smell of sweat and alcohol, I was being asked to switch positions every few minutes.

I had told him to "Stop!" during because he was hurting me; he was strong and had a masculine. Overpowering with force my hands were clenched down to the couch.

I gathered my clothes, left immediately after he fell asleep and ran down the street, it was cold, and snow was halfway melted on the ground. I had to walk home a few miles because.

There were no taxis on the road. It was somewhat dark, and the sun was beginning to rise. It was either a holiday or the weekend. I went home and slept. I had to continue to see him my entire time there, but I just acted normal. He would constantly talk to me about getting with me and us both liking Asian women and liking Japanese Anime.

.

This case was unfounded.

Korean Soldier KATUSA Kim Tae Kwon

Back in the middle of April 2012 I messaged PFC Kwon on Facebook because he "Liked" all my statuses, and I was trying to figure out why this Soldier added me. From then on, we talked for days about our life problems, past and future. Subjects we talked about included the relationship issues I was having, history events of our lives, and his last relationship, and if all worked out and my relationship issues were sorted out that possibly the two of us could be together, but I could never fully like him for I was still in love with someone else.

Our conversations lasted until approximately April 22nd, 2013, when I returned home from emergency leave and brought some gifts back as a token of friendship. That weekend we went on the DMZ (Demilitarized zone) tour with some other Korean and American Soldiers to which included a trip to an outlet store. At the time we began to hold hands, but we were just friends. I specifically told him via messages that we can befriend each other. As my rocky relationship was ending, going on and off or being finalized June 17th, 2013, around 1700 hours because my boyfriend graduated his term of Korean army enlistment contract and became a civilian again.

Kim and I became closer friends, nothing more until one night we had a one-night stand. Our friendship than turned to Friend with Benefits or what he termed "Best Friends" from May until the 3rd week of June. During May to June, we went to karaoke, dining out at least once a week, buying and browsing for Korean traditional dresses called Hanbok, and played in a ravine near his hometown. Throughout this time knowing Kim the initial stages of friendship seemed great until May/June and thereafter when I started to feel threatened and felt that I had to stay in a friendship/relationship with him because he kept guilt tripping me about making him feel bad, his depression and his suicidal ideations.

The week of June 24th, 2013, and before, he kept threatening me, saying he would kill himself If I did not date him, thus being forced into a relationship.

This email he sent me to hang the relationship over my head for me to continue to be forced to stay in it. Kim even told me he wanted to "chop my ex into tiny pieces and throw him in to the ocean". He even went as far as to investigate my phone, which was password protected, without asking, stole addresses, phone numbers, and email of my ex-lover. At the time I felt scared and forced to do something I did not want to do. I then confided in my supervisor about it, and she took care of it, all three of us talked, and she ordered us to have a no contact order.

We did not have any contact in June, until August during UFG (Ulchi Freedom Guardian exercise Military drill) which was approximately ~ August 16th to 19th around 2100 hours or so after coming back from dinner, not knowing my door didn't properly lock and I went to go smoke. I came back to my room pitch and Kim was standing over my bed with his back turned looking into my phone and messages cause when he turned around, he looked mad, started to yell as I went toward my bed and said, "Why would you do this again?". Not knowing what he was talking about. He walked up to me, put his left hand over my right cheek and slapped me in the face.

I was so shocked and fell back into my mobile coat rack and slid down to the floor. I had my hand over my face where he had slap, I could feel the vibration and force of the slap remaining. Then stayed there tearing up, he kneeled and continued to yell at me then tried to rub my face and said, "Sorry." in a whiny ass voice. And my instinct was to slap his hand away. Thinking, "Get away from me!". I told him not to touch me; he tried to stop me from leaving the room then had the nerve to ask if we were still forcefully dating or being friends.

That was the day I started smoking and still was holding my face for two hours before I cried myself to sleep.

This case was unfounded.

KATUSA Kim Part Two (The Assault)

On September 3rd, 2012, around 2440 to 2450 hours Kim came to my room, opened the door, and just came right in, with a black bag and started taking out a hard drive while I hopped out of bed and ran to my computer. He would have only had 10 to 20 minutes then was supposed to leave but he planned to stay the night and I did not want that. As I was putting up my hair, I told him, " I have a knot in my hair, could you help me get it out?". He spent a few minutes combing it out but could not so I gave him permission to do what he could to get it out. Once he got it out, I went back to bed and let him continue working on the laptop. He said the transfer would take 30 minutes.

As I laid in my bed to rest with my stomach down, meaning my back was revealed, I got a solid 5 to 10 minutes of rest before Kim straddled me on my back and started to massage me. Being exhausted I fell asleep quickly, he hopped on me of his own free will, as I just continued to sleep. But then as he was massaging me, he told me to flip over. As I was drifting in and out of consciousness from exhaustion and lack of sleep, I thought he was someone else, so I started groaning the name of my ex-boyfriend June.

"June....June....", faintly but quietly with my eyes closed and flipped over.

At that point he started to massage my collar bone area, chest and then told me it would be better to take my top off because it would make it easier to massage. I sleepily began to take my top off then fell back into a deep slumber. Once he began massaging my chest, he placed his mouth on my breasts and started sucking them then kissed me on my lips. I refused and did not respond nor kiss him back. He continued to kiss my chest then started to make his way down my stomach with his mouth until he got to my vaginal area and began to digitally penetrate me.

I resisted and tightened my legs and pulled away his hand. I did not want to be touched there even worse penetrated. He knew that I was still in love with someone else and only wanted to have my last moments with that person in that way. But Kim insisted. The more I resisted, the more he would keep asking, “No?", and I whispered "No...". Still being tired as I resisted, he began to keep kissing me my breasts repeatedly to formulate a response. I felt like he was trying to weaken my body. I was frozen, lapsed in a time of inescapable harm or potentially death.

Once paralyzed he began to try and pry my legs open, but I locked them, eventually I got tired enough to just let them open, and then he attempted oral sex. I just kept saying June’s name while still half sleepily trying to close my legs, but he used force to keep them open and continued licking, sucking, and using his tongue. When he finally stopped, I was in agonizing pain. He wiped his face, so I decided to lock my legs again. He returned to sucking at my breasts again, and I locked my legs while he began to touch himself and tried to penetrate me with his male appendage, but I kept contracting my legs until eventually I got tired again and let him pry them open again.

Only for him to keep trying to reinsert his male appendage inside of me, at this point I tried to kick him off and used a combative move to thrust him inward than back, he must have thought that gave him the initiative to continue then tried to penetrate me again, but I locked my vaginal area, contracting it as hard as I could to not allow entry. That became tiring too, so I just let him do what he wanted and even turned to my side when he stopped to contract again, he still tried to keep forcing it in. Because I kept saying the other person's name, Kim said, " Pretend that I am him". I told him, "No".

" I only wanted him; I wanted June to be my last, that was important to me", I stated. Kim replied," I want to be your last". If there was one thing, I did not want to happen that night was to be penetrated by anyone any longer that was the one thing I did not want to happen, and he did it. So, I just let him continue. I was even more exhausted, fighting off a combatant, struggling and trying to save my life from danger. What else was I supposed to do?

This case was unfounded.

Hindsight 20/20:

Even 11 years later I still feel betrayed by both militaries. Neither military prosecuted them.

Backlash After Reporting

Under the Command of CPT Bonnet in the 70th Brigade Support Battalion, HHC I was sexually assaulted December 1, 2012. Currently, I had only been in the U.S. Army for about 9 months. Prior to the sexual assault I was picked to be promoted to PFC with a waiver that was already signed, that favorable action was taken away from me.

I was also defamed and humiliated by being made to sleep on a cot at staff duty for the first three days after the assault, gossiped about by staff and peers, could only leave the Battalion, which I lived, if I had an NCO with me. I was denied favorable actions such as going to the Soldier of the month board, promotion. CPT Bonnet threatened and attempted to discharge me on a Chapter 11: Failure to Adapt to the Military after reporting the sexual assault. The command responded with an unwanted behavioral health evaluation.

When I finally could leave the Battalion by myself after being assaulted by our Korean counterparts KATUSA, the assailant's colleagues harassed me for the rest of my tour in Korea and as a result I could not eat in the chow hall. I complained to the chain of command, but nothing was done. For five months I resorted to the Katusa Snack Bar, Popeyes, Burger King attempted another DFAC, but every time I attempted to go in to the DFAC (Dining Facility), I felt a sense of fear, the assailant and his friends were usually in there. I attempted to use battle buddies to shadow me, and they encouraged me to re-enter, but it brought back many memories.

After reporting sexual assault with Kim (September 3, 2013), I was given poor work assignment removed from my position as a Human Resources Specialist and assigned cleaning duties, pick up trash, and put in the orderly room – those are jobs usually given to Soldiers who had been in trouble.

After the report of the second sexual assault and being moved, I still had to work alongside CPL Kim, passing him in the hallways, down the street, at the smoke pit. The unit and other KATUSA's made it awkward, the KATUSA told me they used my first case of rape blurred my name and used it for their class and told KATUSA' "that is why you don't date or mess with American Female Soldiers they will male false claims of sexual assault toward you". None of this is a lie, I was told by KATUSA' after my first assault my incident came up in their training as a warning.

The effect of having to see the perpetrators on a daily, monthly basis, the forms of social retaliation, constant staring and gossiping from roommates fostered a hostile work environment but I still persevered.

I did not even want to report the second rape because of the negative effect and the physical, psychological, and emotional effects that I was unaware of and undiagnosed until four years later. The retaliation of the first one with CID and my unit's mismanagement of the case/care.

I was convinced reporting was the "right way", I took the chance, reported not knowing I would face the rest of my Military career this far "walking on eggshells", having to "lose potential for advancement", and continue to face "social retaliation in", “threats" and later "disciplinary action".

HINDSIGHT 20/20: Only YOU as the victim can decide ultimately to do a Restricted or Unrestricted report. Do not let your chain of command disregard your circumstance or decide what's best for you and you mental health.

6 *JOINT BASE LEWIS MCCHORD, WASHINGTON*

Fort Lewis, Washington

September 12, 2013- I permanently changed stations to Joint Base Lewis-McChord, WA where I was found at the Waller Hall Reception Building. My ride never showed up from the Battalion Staff Duty and to find my unit, my (Battalion Commander) of 1- 229th ARB, recognized my name and escorted me in his truck to the Battalion.

Now pre-arrival to Washington, I was communicating to my new Battalion S1(Supervisor) by email months in advance from South Korea to understand their expectations, how I could get ahead of myself, unit history. My responses usually came from my new NCOIC (Supervisor) and SPC Perkins. The email traffic was my attempt to build a positive relationship with my new unit and rapport.

Once I in-processed 1-229th Attack Reconnaissance Battalion, CID (investigators), the Battalion and Brigade SHARP pulled me aside to talk to me about them knowing I am a sexual assault survivor from South Korea and how my case was still open.

From September 2013 to November 2013, I did not have any disciplinary, work, performance, or family issues. I went on a field training exercise to Idaho called High Altitude Maintenance Exercise, where SFC Morales. and I were the sole S1 (Administration) for that duration of time end of October into November 2013, we returned to Washington state before Thanksgiving. I experienced a few family deaths in November and December of 2013, my divorce was finalized, and I was progressing to where I earned my specialist waiver early and was pinned by SFC Morales December 1, 2013.

SFC M. had called me on the phone during our unit's deployment readiness Soldier Readiness Process (SRP), he was in a rush and needed our files there, at the time I didn't have a car and I relayed the message the same way that was asked of me in an upbeat excited voice, "SGT E., SFC M. says we must leave TIME NOW.", that ended being disrespectful because we were in a rush, and she was taking her time.

I ended up getting counseled twice for this issue and was asked to type up a paper. I submitted the paper late because of internet difficulties and then in a subsequent counseling or being late I was humiliated and disrespected back by being told to repeat every morning for come 0900 to come to the position of attention and recite the Creed of the Noncommissioned Officer.

One morning came and she was down the hall, but the counseling specifically stated I have to say the creed at a certain time. I stood up in an empty office and proceeded to proudly recite the creed. CPL E. interjected loudly from down the hall, stomping into the office, locking me up in parade rest, "SPC Morbeck, I am not in...". As if I am not humiliated already that I am the only Soldier with this type of treatment under her supervision.

I brought the situation of her attitude and treatment to SSG B. and SFC M. and they told me they would talk to her. Nothing resulted from their talk, I was later switched under SSG B. supervision and still had to take orders respectively from CPL E.

SSG B. emphasizes that CPL E. is learning to be an NCO and she still needs to respect her rank and position.

March 29, 2014: The Unit deploys and to prepare the unit I was asked to help with Soldier Readiness Processing, supervising, briefings, and accountability (conducting Personnel Asset Inventories) on my own on multiple occasions.

When the unit deployed CPL E., SPC L., SFC M., CPT Z. deployed. The rear detachment S1 consisted of myself, SSG B., and PFC B.

My NCOIC SFC M. wanted me to deploy with them and originally, I was considered on the list until the Battalion Commander shot the request down and told him I could not deploy with a sexual assault case.

The information that was relayed to me by SSG B. was that I could not deploy because I was sexually assaulted. A week after I reported that to the medical staff CPT R., she called unit 1SG. First Sergeant (1SG) requested me to come in the office and told me I was not allowed to deploy because my sexual assault case was still active. (Hence why I regret telling anyone and reporting the second time around.)

April 2014: Under the Rear Detachment Command of 1SG D. and CPT C. SGT M. and SGT L. were two NCO's leading Physical Training exercises one morning and mocking the Gay community, knowing, or not knowing that we had Gay and Lesbian Soldiers in that formation that morning. During group formation we the comment "Hop if you are GAY" from SGT M. and response from SGT L. "If you are offended go to the woods and pick up some faggots" after I on-the-spot corrected the NCO SGT M. of his inappropriate comments while doing the hamstring stretch standing caused conflict for me. I bring this up because my on the-spot correcting as an E-4 was relayed to the 1SG and Commander as "interfering with unit cohesion" when CPT C. threatened and attempted to Chapter 5-17 me during

August 12, 2014.

Because I reported their comments to the Equal Opportunity sergeant, and he pulled the NCO's aside and talked to them. The next few weeks the NCO's mentioned above and SGT M. wife SGT M. and her NCO started treating me disrespectfully to the point where the female SGT M. would call me after hours on multiple occasions leaving voicemails or calling me yelling for kicking back awards my supervisor told me to return to the company. Even though ten minutes ago she was arguing with SSG B. about it in the office over the phone and I was there.

The other NCO's and peers started to spread rumors about me, and those rumors circulated back to my supervisors, 1SG and Commander. It became another attempt at "undermining my credibility as a Soldier where leaders in my unit and peers didn't take me seriously and mocked me behind my back".

As you continue to see there can be toxic hostile work environments, lack of communication, and Senior Leaders just wanting to sweep this under the rug and cover their own ass.

Fort Lewis, Washington Part Two

I reported these nonstop unnecessary behaviors to 1SG (First Sergeant), and he told me he would talk to them and side with them. While continuing to work in a hostile environment asking for assistance after I was discharged from Intensive Outpatient which I volunteered for, the 1SG and Commander moved our S1 shop to the orderly room while SSG (Supervisor) was on convalescent leave. The 1SG knew I had been harassed by the SGT's in the orderly room for singling me out and for being pregnant. He persisted that 1SG was going to handle it.

I volunteered for the Intensive Outpatient Program treatment for anxiety related issues during pregnancy. I want to clarify that on the medical retirement Standard Form 600 block j, documents "occupational stressors" which was now geared toward Equal Opportunity reporting reprisals and pregnancy mistreatment.

While pregnant I asked my supervisor if I could attend BSEP (ASVAB GT Class), Soldier of the Month boards (asked monthly), and if I could go to an NCOES school prior to being pregnant. At every angle at advancing my career, I have been denied and given no explanation. Both units were aware of my sexual assault cases.

The main issue while attending Intensive Outpatient was while being referred for an unexplainable CDE (Command Directed Evaluation) requested by CPT C. in which he attempted to Chapter 5-17 me first. I was denied the favorable action of taking leave. Acting 1SG and I quote "You had all that time off, and you want more". This was no ordinary request for leave, my husband's mother died a year earlier, and he did not get to visit her grave. My ex-husband wanted to grieve and visit her gravesite in Ashland, Oregon.

After SFC W. reported it to the 1SG and Commander, I

was later told that day when I came home that CPT C. called my husband "First Shirt – Air Force 1SG" and told 1SG DAVIS and my husband that "I didn't want to take leave with him, conveyed that my husband was suicidal" and on top of that violated my HIPPA rights by telling 1SG , " I am planning on chaptering SPC Morbeck for being mentally unstable". The effect CPT C. had on my marriage but negatively impacted. Not to forgot, adding unneeded stress to a pregnant woman.

The command was clearly overstepping their boundaries and creating a hostile work environment. CPT C., sided with the NCO's that were having "issues" with me started exaggerating and fabricated another Command Directed Evaluation with false evidence of collateral misconduct that was submitted and reviewed August 12, 2014, with information about my sexual assault in the primary bullet.

I advocated for myself and counteracted the false information which wiped out the evaluation.

With my reports of sexual assault being used against me by commands to recommend separation is a continuous pattern. The end of August came, and I wrote down all the retaliatory acts so CSM (Supervisor above all the supervisors, Command Sergeant Major) can review them with me after asking him to move me up to HHC, 16 Combat Aviation Brigade S1 on August 29, 2014.

In the beginning my work ethic and performance was above par that 7th Infantry Division wanted to move me up there, with their knowledge of the retaliatory acts and hostile environment while

pregnant CSM R. (My mentor and G1, 7ID), and SGT Bu. (Mentor G1, 7ID) attempted to pull me but 16 CAB CSM resisted. The unit (later found out) told Division they would take care of me.

(Hostile environment due to pregnancy and sexual assault stigma)

The background of how I was admitted to 5N our inpatient Psychiatric Unit: CPT R, SGT M. and I is interesting. All three of us had a meeting, I agreed to let SGT M. to be in there with me as another set of ears. After discussion with CPT R. my options, I volunteered to try 5N. She told us both while we were in the room together that I was not high risk enough. She had to fabricate on the form that my risk was high enough or 5N would not have admitted me.

20 May 2015: SM presented our safety evaluation and reported ongoing thoughts of self-harm and developing plans for suicide. While waiting for her appointment, SM asked staff at the front desk to call Provost Marshall because she did not trust herself to be safe and later told the provider that she should have stayed at 5N for another week and wanted to go back (because COL X., discharged me on a medication that caused adverse side effects that I was experiencing days earlier). In truth, my command was reacting to me and building a packet to separate me from the U.S. Army because I reported my situations and it cause friction or the higher ups to look at my unit. By a Commander having a sexual violence in their unit. The Commander's perspective is that it looks bad on their leadership position. Since I was the scapegoat, they wanted to fabricate information so that I seemed unstable for them process me out instead of allowing me sufficient time to heal and get better.

Upon discharge from 5N the following incidents happened: 1SG R. and CPT U. came to visit me a few days prior to discharge. CPT U. threatened Chapter 5-17 me, broke the news by counseling me that he was going to chapter me.

CPT G. (16 CAB Psychologist), 1SG R., CPT U., CPT C., and a few nurses were present. I held my composure until the end, I did not even have a chance to seek treatment and have a trial of duty.

Whistleblower Retaliation

I was emotional, still had post pregnancy hormones surging through my bloodstream, breast pumping and on Zoloft. By the time I was discharged, a combination of the Zoloft and my pending threatened Chapter 5-17, caused me to pace back and forth through the halls from May 16 through 18th, have insomnia, especially the last day I was there and waiting for command to come. My brain and body were not functioning well that day, I never had a sense of "fear, paranoia, fixation with doors, a feeling of being afraid of how my unit would receive me and how my body was reacting on Zoloft, caused the female Dr. who examined for PPD (Post Partum Depression) look in my eyes while I was sobbing, shaking, paranoia and asking, "Why do you look so scared?". I was scared because of the medication reaction but even more because of my mistreatment within my unit.

That experience affected my career negatively, interfered negatively with my marriage, and was why I was later referred to a Medical Board and was the whole basis to Medical Retention Control Point.

I was hospitalized again less than 48 hours later due to adverse side effects from the medication causing this time "morbid suicidal thoughts ", spacing out, confusion and almost causing a vehicle collision with a semi-truck which my Commanders held over my head. After reporting to Command about the collision, I told them I did not feel safe driving. The medication impaired my ability to function which the current and former company command team used as a basis to type up the narrative new CDE after I appealed them twice and the

Commander Statement attached to the Medical Board. I was impaired by the Zoloft for the duration of being back to work after release of discharge and for those 48 hours I was judged, counseled multiple times both times I was discharged and stripped of my desk, counseled that my security clearance would possibly be suspended, unassigned from my position and placed in the orderly room as a form of retaliation (supervision), and consistently being accused of unrelated misconduct in order to give me counseling and threatened that if I "continued" that I would receive another Article 15 and that they would press for unfavorable action.

The "demonstrated manipulative behaviors that interfered with unit cohesion" was about me exercising my right as a Soldier to seek out support and character letters, I was also verbally counseled don that and the Command team did not agree with what I was doing, told me I was interfering with the mission when I was asking Soldiers of all ranks that knew me and supported me staying in. I was told that I am not allowed to ask the Soldiers on duty hours, that I would have to call them on my off time. But my Commander had already pulled my clearance, restricted me from computer access and refrained me from being in S1 around PII (Personal Identifiable Information), phone numbers and names account as PII. \

If the other documents were read, you found out that Article 15 of Failure to Report was really an act of reprisal for contacting Inspector General about my pregnancy mistreatment. The other pregnant Soldiers got to go home early and released from duty, but I had to stay long hours after my shift. As a result, I developed hypertension and had to be induced early. My daughter was a 33 + hour labor.

In my defense about the "constant command attention and direct supervision", correct me if I am wrong, it is standard Military protocol after being discharged from an inpatient facility, the act of "direct supervision" was a tactic put in place for unwarranted physical visits to meet up with supervisors that the commander put in place and agreed upon for about two weeks or so. Unnecessary, I was not actively suicidal, if they were that concerned keeping me in the barracks would have been an easier choice.

I appealed two Command Directed Evaluation one by CPT E. and MAJ D.

Somewhere in my file my "credibility" is short because I am just judged off past medical history and not considered the tenacity, resiliency and progress I have made these last few years. In my commands I am not taken seriously or respected due to this stigma and my leadership potential. Despite the stigma, I still persevere am positive, motivated, tenacious, hardworking and that scares people with the potential these Soldiers keep telling me I have but not allowing me to advance.

Looking through just the one four-page document of the Medical Evaluation Board, I was allegedly accused of:

5 retaliatory Command Directed Evaluations (Mandated Mental Health Exam)

3 threats of Chapter (1 – Chapter 11: Failure to Adapt and 2 – Chapter 5-17: means you had a physical or mental condition that prevented you from fulfilling your Military duties.) 1 attempted Medical Evaluation Board and Physical Evaluation Board

For a fact I was diagnosed with an anxiety disorder from South Korea to until 1 June 2015.

That evidence contradicts the label of "chronic

adjustment disorder". I was not diagnosed with a "chronic adjustment disorder" until after the medical board examination which I appealed at all levels numerous times trying to prove my Commands mistreatment. Signs do not add up, I can see foul play within the text. The Military behavioral health system should not be allowed to say I was treated. My command while in South Korea, when I initially came to Washington, and we were preparing for deployment and when I was pregnant was being told not to go to my appointments and to cancel them or reschedule due to the needs of the mission. There is more to the situation than just these medical files. I prepared this document to make sense of the whole story.

Note: The Military will use "adjustment disorder" to not fully compensate you for PTSD, make sure to get a second opinion and answer the PTSD questions truthfully when you are asked about it during treatment or if you're forced to see Behavioral Health). As you feel right now, I was scared to answer them honestly and if I had to do redo it now, I would have made sure even though I fear being discharged that it is important if you need to challenge your command and appeal. Why? Because it creates a trail of documented evidence you can use to appeal or get adequate treatment if you want to be retained.

At the time I wrote "I would like to be reevaluated not based off inaccurate medical record, and a reconsideration for proper treatment of my accurate medical diagnosis changed from "adjustment disorder" to "PTSD secondary to Military Sexual Assault."

If this was not important to me and I felt I could lose this case, or if I was just making up stuff, then I would not have a chance. These words are true. I may not be finished yet on this document completely, here is what I have compiled."

To date, I had over 20 letters of recommendation from all over my community and other Chain of Command from Colonel, Chief Warrant Officer, Sergeant First Class, Staff Sergeants, Sergeants, and all ranks advocating on my behalf to retain me and allow me to get help.

PFC Ramos (Warrior Transition Battalion)

Now is the time to tell the story about the numerous sexual assaults while in Fort Lewis, Washington. Although I do not have the investigations of them with me, I will do my best to relay by memory these fragments of details. We have unknown Soldier, PFC Ramos, CPT Delacruz, and SGT Eli.

To the unknown Soldier who forever will be etched in my mind, and whose stories I forgot because I blocked out. I do not forgive you. I just do not remember because it was that insignificant.

I met PFC Ramos outside by the smoke pit one night while I was on staff duty, (24-hour security detail), he was fidgeting with his cell phone talking about how it was in Korean and how he just came back from there. I instantly used that to build rapport and told him I could help fix it. I told him when I was finished with staff duty or on my next break, I would help him reprogram his phone from Korean to English and he gave me his room number. I did not think anything of it but that I was going to help a Soldier.

Time passes by and my Sergeant releases me for a few hours to get some sleep, so I go and help that Soldier using all ways nondetectable to reach his room and going counterclockwise to reach him. That was my first premonition. Once I reached his barracks room, I knocked, and he let me in. He was laying down watching a movie. I asked him to give me his phone. Reprogrammed it and then he asked me to stay. In the back of my head, I felt that I should have left.

He invited me over to sit on the edge of the bed and the next thing I know he is on top of me, and my uniform is being stripped off me, slightly delirious and confused. My newly fresh operational camouflaged patterned uniformed is being shredded right between my eyes with the figure of a Hispanic man above me. I, on my back, him on top of me unable to move, pinned down him trying to penetrate me. Unforeseen, hopeless, distraught, and once again feeling destroyed.

My mind zoned out, I was not in my body, this time. I disassociated, too many of these attacks and frozen. They compound. Why was this happening yet again? I do not remember much of the attack. Just what I was feeling. I felt scared, powerless, empty, a shell. INVISIBLE, a tool, someone only used for sexual activities. And that is how I continued to perceive myself for an exceptionally long time, 9 years to be exact. This case was Unfounded.

Captain Delacruz

I met Captain Delacruz through a phone application called Whisper. I posted a Whisper about being raped in the Military and how they were kicking me out. He responded trying to console me. We ended up meeting at a bar downtown in Tacoma on 6th avenue called The MIXX (a Gay bar).

I had arrived early that night not planning on meeting anyone, had a few drinks and sitting on a bar stool at the bar. I gave the bartender the keys and instinctively told him, "If I try to leave, I'm not driving". While four or five drinks in I was still texting this stranger through Whisper, he wanted to meet up and chat in person, so he met me at the bar. When he arrived, he pulled up next to me and started feeding me more drinks. Eight drinks go by, I am singing karaoke, getting up to go to the bathroom and finding out my drink has been replaced with another drink. He has been giving me the same pink strawberry milkshake drug induced drink all night.

Hours go by, he walks me outside to his car, I tell him I want to check the other bar down the street and that I am hungry. Stumbling out the bar, staggering down the sidewalk. He leads me to his car and hauls me away to his to an RV park where he lives in a trailer. Halfway cognizant I step inside pushing past a metal jagged door, looking around me with shoes, uniforms, and junk lying across the floor, he walks me toward the bed.

I hit the bed instantly and my eyes closed shut. I could feel the bare hands of this man peeling each article of clothing off my skin, pulling up my skirt just enough, pulling down my shirt just enough.

When is enough, enough? I thought. I was barely

coherent. Drugged, inebriated, and cold lying in an unknown stranger's bed being raped for what felt like an eternity. He had to wake up early the next day so after the assault, I passed out completely until he woke me up to take me back to my car.

The next morning, I woke up with a pounding headache and everyone acted like nothing happened until I safely made it back to my car. Let me tell you, I did the walk of shame to my car, opened the door, and sat down. Tears instantly began gushing down my face, I knew something had happened. My body ached in pain, my vaginal area bruised and sore, my mind incomprehensible. Guess what I thought..."Why did this happen again, and again and again?".

I immediately reported it to my chain of command and went to Madigan to get the rape kit done.

At this time, I was juggling two rape cases and this case happened three days before I got out of the Military. In the process of this, I participated in a workshop for service members struggling with mental health issues. The workshop is called ***I WAS THEIR*** film workshop. It was created to help those struggling with mental health issues tell their story in a short film. I do not want to release my real name, but it does exist. A year later I worked at Pierce College, and they had my short film on display in their psychology and Criminal Justice class. I walked in and saw it on the bulletin board and was so amazed.

From then on, I decided to use my public speaking skills as an advocate for Military Sexual Violence and taught a seminar as a panel, with my short film, and shared my story to class about 30 individuals. I would like to continue my advocacy once I retire from law enforcement.

This was found and he was sentenced to adulatory and discharged from the Military.

His command downgraded his sexual assault charge.

Sergeant Eli

I met Sergeant Eli, a Palauan American Soldier, at the Warrior Zone on North Fort Lewis some time ago before the incident took place January 19th, 2017. I was just getting off duty from work as a Federal Correctional Officer when I received a text from Sergeant Eli asking if he could come over because he did not want to drive back to base drunk and get a DUI. Knowing my leadership history and kindness for helping Soldiers, I invited him over to stay the night. The report reads:

By the time I fell completely asleep it was approximately 2400 hours.

I woke up at 0130 after he left and told my roommate, "I think I was just violated in my sleep'". The seaman was dripping out of me as I stood there. Then I fell back asleep and woke up around 0400 hour to get ready for work and left. I thought nothing of it until 1020 hours when I went to my car to check my phone.

At 1020 hours SGT Eli text me," Are you still on that birth control thing?"

Me: "Yeah, why do you ask? Did something happen last night?" Eli: "Yes, do you or do you not?"

Me: "I do have an IUD, but what happened? Is it sharp related? Cause I'm quite sure I said I didn't want to have sex because I had with the prosecutor and reliving my other sexual assault account alongside an inmate dying at work".

Eli: Are you mad?

Me: Fucking of course, I am mad, as soon as I said no, and you

did it anyway while I was sleeping. When you wanted to come over to "sleep" because you were drunk and "tired". I woke up naked when I had my gear, underwear, and bra on.

How can anyone consent in my sleep?

After the message exchange I reported it to the Officer at work who directed me to HR, I then called the VA and my Special Victims attorney and the local police. I reached Madigan at 1800 where I met my attorney, CID agents, Victim Advocate, and a SANE nurse for rape kit.

The actual rape:

I stayed in bed as he entered at approximately 2130ish. I figured it was him and I remained sleeping. He entered my house and my bedroom with the lights off. He undressed and entered my bed with only his boxers and immediately started attempting to place my hand on his male appendage, I gravely and quickly moved my hand away. He then kissed me on my neck and tried to kiss my lips, but I turned.

After turning he wet his fingers and digitally penetrated me with his left-hand numerous times as he kept attempting, I would shuffle. After the third time; hazily asleep; I yelled," Touch me again, and I'll handcuff you and pepper spray you". At approximately 2330 my roommate came home, and I got out of bed and turned the lights on to talk to her. She put the music on and turned on all the lights. I alerted her he was there then blatantly talked loud enough for him to here, while he hid under the covers pretending to sleep.

I talked to her for approximately 20 minutes, put my entire correctional officer uniform on, belt, vest, boots included then laid back down. He appeared asleep. I slept in uniform for about ten minutes, then took most of it off until I was back in my underwear and bra. By that time, I fell asleep due to the sleeping medication in my system.

"List of charges per UCMJ (Uniformed Code of Military Justice) Article 120:

Specification 1:

In that Sergeant Eli, US Army, did, at or near Tacoma,

Washington on or about January 19th, 2017, commit a sexual act upon her by penetrating her vulva with his finger, by causing bodily harm to her, to wit: penetrating her with his finger, without her consent, with an intent to gratify the sexual desire of himself.

Specification 2:

In that Sergeant Eli, US Army, did, at or near Tacoma, Washington on or about January 19th, 2017, commit a sexual act upon by penetrating her vulva with his finger, when he reasonably should have known that she was asleep, with an intent to gratify the sexual desire of himself.

Specification 3:

In that Sergeant Eli, US Army, did, at or near Tacoma, Washington on or about January 19th, 2017, commit a sexual act upon by causing penetration of her vulva with his male appendage when he reasonably should have known that she was asleep. He had caused fear the day after when he texted her at work January 20th, 2017 - as he texted her about the incident."

After the fact when I would see him on post within the last three months, he would cause fear by anxiety that he could hurt me again. I was afraid that he would come to find me now that he was discharged from the Military and remained in the same county.

The assailant was discharged from the US Army on January 28th, 2018, at 1700 hours. Atlas we have at least two victories.

This case was founded, and we almost went to trial, but he decided to get out on a chapter and was kicked out of the Military.

7 Parenting struggles and Divorce After Trauma

My daughter has lived on and off with her foster mother since she was 8 months old due to my ex-husband's abusive nature (psychologically and mentally). When she was eight months old, D. and I were both active-duty Military members. He had factually placed a gun up to his face while sitting on the couch and pulled the trigger then took the same weapon and placed a round to fire at the television and threw himself down the stairs. The day after I voluntarily placed my daughter into Child Protective Services with the Army's help. At the time I was active-duty Army and was suffering from postpartum depression and untreated/unknown Post Traumatic Stress Disorder from my multiple sexual assaults from the Military. I placed Ariana in the custody of the mother and gave my rights over to her in December 2019. For legal reasons, I can not elaborate on this so I will omit this. Just know it is possible to recover.

To date in 2023 of December, I finally received my veteran section 8 housing, relocated to Philadelphia called Duffield Veterans Village. Which is a newly funded 42 room apartment haven for Veterans and reunited with my daughter 2 years ago.

I am so grateful.

8 The Aftermath

The aftermath is about the struggle between transitioning from the Military to homelessness, domestic violence, regaining employment, Veteran Affairs, college and returning to the civilian work force. It was by no means easy for me. This timeframe lasts from September 2015 to March 2021.

From September 2015 to April 2016, I transitioned to the medical unit called the Warrior Transition Unit. In between that struggle I was going through divorce, my daughter in child protective services and beginning the transition from Military to civilian not to mention that sexual assaults in between. I finally left a hostile command and came into a richer healing environment. As the time drew near to discharging, I ended up homeless with no job in sight.

Note that I was still legally married to my ex-husband, and I asked him if I can stay with him, but I ended up living in my car for the next six months, then being subsequently homeless for years on end on and off until 2019 of March. Those were turbulent times indeed. From night to night, I would sleep in my car in various location from my ex-husband's truck to Walmart parking lot and on post secretly, while gaining part-time employment at Dominoes on North Fort Lewis and going full time to online college to finish my degree. I also took the time to go to the gym.

Six months went by, and I ended up getting a security job, moving into Veteran Affairs section 8 housing program and graduating from college.

Until I got in to law enforcement and Sergeant Eli came

along, then I flew back to Wisconsin for a year from February 2018 to February of 2019. From Wisconsin, I stayed in the Boudicca House, which was a female shelter for veterans, landed another security job and spent several months working on getting into the Police Academy. My dream was coming to fruition, and I was content, until the case came up for Captain Delacruz and halted my Police Academy process. I ended up leaving the Police Academy and moving back to Washington state to be with my daughter.

I spent those four years trying to rebuild my life after discharge and trauma. Having over eight jobs, and moving from place to place, unstable lover to lover... Once I finally came back to Washington state in 2019 of March, I stayed in the fun, small, town of Soldier's Home in Orting, Washington. I stayed there for a few months and then moved in with a Marine veteran and his friend. Living with two unknown males, once which I met at the Veteran Affairs during group therapy was a process. In time, it too, became hostile and intrusive. I fled, was homeless again. If I could count on my hand, I would use both hands to tell you how many times I was homeless, that goes for how many civilian jobs I have also had since transitioning.

I did not gain stable housing on my own until December of 2019, and stable long-term employment until March of 2019 until December 23,2020 then due to the pandemic lost both of those opportunities. Now I am just a full-time mother focusing on my self-healing journey, public speaking opportunities and my daughter.

9.1 Military Sexual Trauma and Dating

Now this chapter focuses on sexual dysfunction, romance after trauma, my experiences, and some issues no one is willing to tread on.

For a long time, I lied to men and women when I would l sleep with them about "getting me off". I am sexually incapable of feeling orgasms due to my sexual assaults back than, but I am starting to open up.

Dating is extremely difficult because I used to share my information of my rapes from the Military upfront, either subconsciously trying to self-sabotage or hoping they would just love me for me. I know some of you reading can relate. Dating is not easy. What is even more excruciatingly painful is that I have a daughter and I want to tell her my story but as a mother and given her age of nine, she is too young to know.

I want to teach her, inform her, protect her, and guide her. This book is partly being written for her just in case one day I am no longer around she will have this memento of me. Trust, trust is a big issue. I am scared to tell new partners about my traumas, triggers during sex, because I want to seem normal. But if they trigger me then they see the opposite of what I wanted.

Some of my triggers used to be my hair being pulled, being slapped on the ass, and being choked in any fashion.

Other triggers could be someone grabbing me on the shoulders from behind, or from below on my hips from behind. Sensory reminders of the trauma, certain smells, sights, darkness, things of that nature.

I pay attention to my body's danger signals and used to ignore them to appear normal. That is not healthy. Healing from sexual trauma is a gradual, ongoing process. My healing journey and process is different from yours and others, it is not linear. It is all over the place. Setbacks, one step forward, two steps back. I commonly like to talk about my trauma and will to just about anybody. It is not a secret; it is not primitive. It is not even something I feel I should hide.

People get taken back, scared, flabbergasted, and even turned off by how much I can talk about it so openly.

That does not mean you have too. Some of my deepest secrets with my trauma involve opening to people too quickly and my relationships or first dates fizzling out with no repair. Or sexual relationships, like having multiple unhealthy one-night stands with too many strangers off dating applications like Tinder, OK Cupid, and Whisper. I meet people with potential than have the habit of habitually ruining it right away. I do not want you to fall into the same pitfall unprotected sex and getting pregnant multiple times over the past few years which involved in miscarriages and one abortion. I was homeless at the time and did not feel I could bring the baby into the world in that condition.

Sexual Trauma has a funny way of bringing the worst out of you. At those times I already regarded myself as damaged goods and unwanted or only seeking attention through sex that I did not fully value myself. I did not have boundaries. I have never told anyone these most vulnerable facts. In fact, it is embarrassing but they are part of the history and trauma, thus need to be told.

SIDENOTE: Over time this will change. The more treatment for mental health and going the Veterans Affairs Military Sexual Trauma groups, Warrior Renew, Dialectical Behavior Therapy, Cognitive Behavioral Therapy, Intensive Outpatient, PTSD Clinic, Exposure Therapy, and other healing modalities can help. I have experiences inpatient and outpatient treatment and have the skills to cope on my own now.

I am not a licensed mental health professional, but I am an advocate. This list is not intended to frighten the reader for these have been my past experiences.

9.2 Military Sexual Trauma, Mental Health and Suicidality

The first time I ever had suicidal thoughts was after my first actual rape with KATUSA Ji after my command locked me in my room for three days and on that cot back in 2012 of December.

The second time was dealing with post-partum depression in 2015 March after I gave birth to my daughter.

Then subsequently it went on unnoticed for many years, festering, like and unseen wound.

Once I came to realization that I had PTSD in November of 2015, my suicidality became worse, but it was always hidden. Deep inside, deep in the crevices of my mind. Unable to escape both what had happened to me and what my mind chose to relive on a constant basis. The fear, the anguish, the mental pain, the disassociation. I was numb, cold, just a hollow shell.

Once I realized I had PTSD due to Military Sexual Trauma, I started to understand why I was feeling all these intrusive memories, mostly thoughts, and deepened intense emotional states.

I have journeyed through a few rehabilitation centers to help heal from Madigan, Well-found, Fairfax and Veteran Affairs. I have found them useful as far as coping skills and learning to redirect my overwhelming feelings from the past into more creative outlets.

Throughout the years of 2016 to 2020 the Veteran Affairs and civilian hospital gave me medications that counteracted each other which caused adverse effects in my body on multiple occasions: which was worsened suicidal ideations. Until March to April 2020 when I was given Prozac and that caused a myriad of suicide behaviors.

Having similar empathy changed my life for the better and made me humble. I still tend to beat myself up a little, but I am learning to nurture myself more and not be so hard on myself. At the time I was seeing a psychiatrist at the VA for medication and weight loss management, and an outside referral for EMDR at the VA choice program for psychotherapy. I have been doing this on and off for the last 6 years and it has helped. I have also delved into non-western healing modalities like shamanic healing and soul retrieval. It is imperative or important to continue a constant method of healing in whatever you choose, be it nature, therapy.

As a result, I learned I was hospitalized from April 19, 2020, to April 22, 2020 at St Claire's medical center in Lakewood, WA. Within 30 minutes my speech was slurred, I blacked out. I do not remember anything but waking up on the 21st of April. The nurses and Doctor advised me I went into intensive life saving measures and "respiratory failure", woke up intubated with an induced coma and in my own comatose. I had a major life changing "metaphysical death" and near-death experience, left my rucksack and full battle rattle over on the other side and crossed back over reborn, renew, healed, serene peace washed over me. A new sense of life and now all these positive changes and turning of the wheel. (DO NOT ATTEMPT!!!)

That was not even a reflection of me. In my right mind without coercion from those medications I would never have done that rationally. How would YOU survive? Learn from my mistakes, challenges, and life. If I can survive and save at least one person directly or indirectly; I have accomplished this task.

On April 19, 2020, at approximately 1657 hours or thirty minutes prior I was triggered from a one-night stand on my MST PTSD, was induced on psychiatric medication Zoloft (primary), which I advised them not to give me in the civilian inpatient setting. I was told if I did not comply, I would not be allowed to leave if I did not take the medication. I was overmedicated with Clonazepam (1 MG Tablet (60), Fluoxetine (Prozac) 40 MG, (60), Haloperidol 10 MG, (60), Olanzapine 5 MG, (60), Ondansetron 4 MG (60), Propranolol 10 MG (60), and finally Quetiapine (300 MG) (60). From April 19 to the 22nd I was hospitalized, then hospitalized.

Imagine this: What do you think the total amount of mg of pills that I took? 22,200 mg of psych meds and one soju Prozac skips the process of thinking and that buffer to take a step back and if you have PTSD or other mental health or emotional challenges; causes you to go straight to Suicidal Behavior and Actions (i.e. Attempts). Needs to be discontinued in America. The infamous hospital was Wellfound Behavioral Health in Tacoma, WA.

10 VETERAN HOMELESSNESS

I was chronically homeless from the day I left the military April 13, 2016 with spurts of apartments here and there. From living in the car, to sleeping on a beach under a Banyan Tree in Hawaii or on the chilling beaches of Venice beach.

It is embarrassing to write this on paper, but it needs to be said because it is part of the history of aa homeless female veteran. It is imperative to understand that the bulk of my confidence and autonomic survival behaviors are engrained from all the combined military training classes and invoking the grit that courses through my veins.
I want my daughter to know that no matter how intense and hurtful life can be, learning resiliency and inner fortitude are important traits to evolve as a human. Mommy never asked for any of this trauma or these bad things to happen to her.

Mommy spent 6 or 7 years on and off trying to get help for my mental health from my injuries in the military. In the height of the pandemic, I traveled from Seattle to New Jersey in May 2021 to do a welfare check on my daughter. Needless to say, I was also going through a spiritual awakening that and after driving 21 days with minimal food, no gas, sleeping in the car and driving as legally fast as I could I made it to Mount Holly, New Jersey and Fort Dix McGuire Lakehurst. Since they didn't let me see her by law after a week I left and turned my car in, left it at the airport and flew to Hawaii.

In that moment of despair and desperation of not being able to see my daughter I threatened my life to make sure she was safe and was locked away in Virtua hospital in New Jersey for a week or two. I never meant to say what I said but in that moment of missing my daughter and driving 21 days with minimal resources to make sure she was safe metaphorically crushed me inside. If only my daughter had known the tribulations and trials of what I endured to protect her.

Now on to Hawaii. After being released from the hospital and sleeping in car for multiple days on end. I spent my next Veteran Disability check on flying to Hawaii thinking it would be a haven away from my abuser enough time to find housing and heal. Let me tell you, being homeless in Hawaii is very daunting. Since it was 2021 and Covid was still an ongoing issue when I arrived in Oahu, Hawaii I had to quarantine for two weeks in a hostile with no access to the outside. After two weeks I was released and on my own getting to explore, know the people, visit sacred areas and spend time in the ocean during the day. At night, I would sleep with my old hanbok (Korean dress) layered on top of me to hide my while I slept under a huge banyan tree which had enough shelter to cover my body while I slept with my belonging tied to my leg for a whole month.

Once the month was up and I received my monthly stipend from the VA (Veteran Affairs) I flew back home to Seattle-Tacoma, Washington to find out I still had my apartment and let a veteran I met in the hospital stay there because he had legal trouble. I was then later betrayed by him. Lesson learned. Then once that lease was up I moved to Los Angeles, California from August 2021 until April of 2022 when I met Jay Park again.

Los Angeles, California was an interesting life lesson and opportunity. When I arrived, I admitted myself to the Veteran Affairs hospital inpatient unit to see if I could get housing resources quicker or go inpatient for treatment. Soon that was the wrong thing to do because they made me sign a 6-year affidavit to not use firearms which meant I couldn't apply for the jobs I wanted such as Law Enforcement or Armed Security.

I was so disappointed in myself, if only I could find stability. If only I could get a handle on my life. I began to wonder if I really was the screw up that my family and daughter immediate family always said I was. However, they never went through what I did specifically. As I meandered around Venice Beach in California for a week or so sleeping under the bay watch towers that lifeguards used during the night while falling asleep to the waves. As I recall that time frame tears fall from my face. There are only a handful of times I thought of my daughter and sobbed a horrifying wail of agony and tears that could drown out the ocean while screaming at the top of my lungs and gasping for air as I slept under the watch tower on the beach. I would miss her with all my heavy heart but thought I was a failure and thought she would be better without me. I then would wander the beach suicidally wanting to throw myself in the ocean only to be mauled by sharks. It was a dangerous thought process.

I knew I had to get help, so I used public transportation to Long Beach to get help with housing. I didn't want to really die, not again. I just wanted to be out of that situation. I often wondered how I could face my daughter or if I'd ever be able to see her again. The police had told me before I left New Jersey that there was a protection order against me, and I couldn't contact my daughter until it was resolved. So, I went my separate ways until I was able to resolve it on April 8th, 2022.

Back to Los Angeles. The Veteran Affairs process for housing took almost a year or so to acquire which meant I had to maintain my homeless status until housed. I ran in to some male veterans who befriended me and told me I could stay at their places only to get used, drugged, raped and almost killed this time. That was a wake-up call. Just because someone is labeled a veteran doesn't mean you can automatically trust them. After those frightful events I knew it was time to turn my ego down a couple notches. After all what could I lose, I already had lost everything. I went to the police station the next day explained what happened and they sent me to a Women Day Center that immediately housed me in a Women's Church Shelter in Filipino town district of Los Angeles for which I stayed for almost a year until I left in April.

In November of 2021 I met Charlie Ikeda. He had Autism/Aspergers like my younger brother and that resonated with me. I often walk to Little Tokyo and record Tik Toks. Often people would come up to me while I was filming and that is how I met Charlie. He is significantly older than me, but he had the resources to help me which I am grateful for. I felt a sense of rapport from him since he reminded me of the younger brother I had raised. I am beyond grateful to Charlie and his mom for treating me as their own despite my circumstances. We are all still close and I often visit his mom and him yearly to reunite. Thank you for all the fond memories, Charlie and his mom.

As you see, I have been homeless in Seattle, Hawaii, Wisconsin, Los Angeles, Philadelphia for quite a few years after the military. Each time I did my best to get out of those situations and seek physical and mental health help. This was the life of a rape survivor from the military as a female and I am sure there are, were and will be many more like me. That is why it is imperative to see this book to the end. My motto is, **"If I can survive these events, so can you"**. There is always hope. Find the silver lining.

After I met Jay Park again in April of 2022 to thank him in person for saving my life, I then flew to Philadelphia to be closer to my daughter and reintegrate into her life. As soon as I arrived at Philadelphia International Airport, I contacted the Michael J. Crescent Veterans Affairs hospital and went inpatient again to work with social workers to start the process yet again for housing. They sent me to a Women Haven female veteran home near the VA where I stayed for a few months until they shut down. I continued to work with the VMC (Veterans Multi-Service Center) in downtown Philadelphia until I got accepted into housing the following year later.

I know this book will reach those that need it. It is not just a testimony but a life lesson of not wanting fellow survivors to fall into the same pitfalls. Learn from my mistakes and hardships.

11 SPIRITUALITY AND JAY PARK

I was hesitant to leave this chapter out due to past fear of criticism. When I do live interviews, I often give thanks to Jay Park and let the interviewer know the positive life changing impact he made on me in April of 2016 when I left the military. So… Who is Jay Park and how does he induce healing?

I met Jay Bum Park five days after I was released from the military in Seattle, WA April 17, 2016. During that time my daughter was in foster care. I was processing the trauma. Homeless in my car. Jobless. Mentally exhausted from being undiagnosed with anxiety and PTSD and wanting to commit suicide after his concert. I did not necessarily know too much about him other than learning some of the music while I was stationed in South Korea. I was lost. Although it's a blur now, he basically was kind to me, and they gave me a STAFF pass because I helped organize their lines prior to the event. Took a personal photo with the AOMG musicians by myself but normally it was grouped. A plethora of kindness was bestowed upon me, and I went home the next day alive until my accident on April 19, 2020.

So…. Vanessa, how does this all connect? Fast forward to the coerced medically induced Suicide attempts I woke up in a comatose in the ICU induced with a tube down my throat and as I was opening my eyes, I felt the most peaceful energy light up my entire body. I felt a sense of renewal. From that point on it was still COVID Pandemic so I was released home and scrolling social media and paid someone for a portrait of my "Soulmate". And that is when I thought of him. The portrait looked exactly like Jay Park and as she described him and gave me the sketchy and a blurb in the email. I started to look him up December of

2020.

I tried to dismiss it and was skeptical until I started doing research on the concept of soul mates and found other topics. Such as the modern spiritual terms. I started googling angels, spirituality, Seraphim, anything to gain wisdom and spiritual knowledge in this situation. BANG!!! That started my healing and spiritual journey to who I am today.

I googled anything from the Twin Flame universe that I could. Past lives, Karmic, all the different types of Spiritual Partners. Having balance of spiritual health, physical fitness, a stable home, therapy if it is needed and Inpatient.

The next few paragraphs are going to sound like Sci-Fi movie and in no way intended to sway the reader toward my beliefs. I am just expressing my personal experiences on this journey to balance and self-love with myself.

Other modalities I loved learning about, and implementing was Reiki (Energy Work), the daily process f taking my power back, egg cleanses, praying, daily walking meditations and using hertz, binaural beats, frequencies and subliminal self-concept audios on YouTube. Finally, many detachments subliminal, overnight audios of self-concept affirmations. Shadow Work and ancestral karma clearing etc.

I didn't necessarily believe this type of concepts but as I kept aligning myself and learning how to pray or manifest than stepping back and following God or Universes nudges intuition to just be in the present moment. At that time, I lived in Seattle/Tacoma, Washington. Moved locations. Burnt my eyes with Epson salt. Traveled the country to make sure my daughter was safe.

My car broke down during my travels. It was a critical time in my healing journey. I was the most unstable mental health wise but spiritually I felt the Universe was guiding me on this journey to strip me away of all my comforts of life to teach me to sustain my own self. Most spiritual folk know this is a spiritual awakening or Dark Night of the Soul. With a combination of my masculine grit from the military, education and my willingness to be open minded and love of learning. I taught myself to not give up and persevere even if I was mentally breaking down. My heart sank as I sped down the interstate to ensure the safety of my daughter after my child loss earlier that month.

Within a span of several years on paper this was my history….

Chronological impact to date for being a Survivor of Sexual Violence:

1. Survivor of Sexual Violence (2011 to 2017 (US. Army), 2019 to 2022 Dec (Post-military)
2. Divorce x2 (2012, 2016)
3. Domestic Violence Survivor (2015, 2016, 2017x 2, 2020, 2022-2023)
4. Homelessness Veteran (2016 to 2023)
5. Being estranged from my daughter to get treatment
6. Financial and employment loss
7. Discrimination in the workforce in civilian and Law Enforcement (2017 until current)
8. Death of four of my five children (2018 December/2019 March/ 2021 February 27/ 2023 March)
9.
10. Suicide/Near Death Experience Survivor (April 19, 2020)

I know, I know my life looks intense. That is not the extent of it. I had to spend three or four years intensely working on myself, ego, getting into spiritual alignment and balance.

I am so happy and at peace with myself. I held on to my belief in faith, scripting, journaling about what my life wanted to look like. Learning to trust my intuition. I came to terms and peace with all of myself. There are still days that I have off days and break down or cry, are irked but the gym helps me.

In 2022 of April, I was living in a shelter in Los Angeles waiting for housing to be available. I moved to California to pursue career of being in the entertainment industry as a public speaker and influencer. I am grateful for the positive kind caretakers in the Church Shelter I lived in. Within the shelter I had my own room which helped to mediate and visualize, manifest my spiritual practices which helped me stay mentally grounded despite the lack of resources.

Be it Universe/God/Angelic being/Energy etc, however you choose to call your version of Higher Power aligned me with the financial blessing to see Jay Park in Florida who attended the UFC 273 between The Korean Zombie & V. My intuition was pushing me to go there.

I felt like the Universe was energetically pushing me to take a leap of faith to get a chance to redeem myself to Thank Jay Park for saving my life. To date, I have interacted with Jay Park in Head in the Clouds event in August of 2022. Subsequently, I have visited him several times at events in 2023. Won Soju Tour in September in Seattle, New York. Followed by The Korean Zombie Pop up in California on November 15. And ended the year being invited to South Korea for the holidays.

Just my thoughts on this situation:

When I was reintroduced to him and thanked him at the UFC fight, I gave him a letter, Dior Sauvage cologne, and a necklace. Throughout the year of 2022 he had worn that necklace often even though he didn't personally reach out to me that gave me the motivation to keep healing and becoming a better person. The Universe (God) for me always works out in my favor and helped me learn that I can create my own success and reality. I kept incorporating the Law of Attraction a Universal Laws to "manifest" our meetings and my desires in life.

Last month at the UFC event for the Korean Zombie, I had a suspicious incline that Jay was going to appear, and the Universe internally nudges me to see him evolve. I had expressed that my grandfather passed away, asked to collaborate, and planted a seed to potentially be in his closer personal circle.

He gives me a sense of hope and I am eternally grateful for him and all his kind interactions with me throughout the last few years.

If you ever read this Jay, I unconditionally love you. You energetically pushed me along the way and guided me during my spiritual awakening. I have been on this healing inner self since my accident in 2020. I know consciously you don't know this but on an energetic spiritual basis you have been tremendously helpful in keeping me on a journey to come into union with you.

My personal internal healing journey is my experience, but those who have had similar experiences will resonate with them. If this doesn't interest, feel free to skip this part.

I can't teach you that part of the life, all humans have to go through there own experience to choose to heal or stay stuck in there current mindset. Thank you so much Jay Park. I appreciate us exisitng in the same Universal space. You are such a beautiful shining soul even though you are healing internally. Please have the courage and strength to ask for help if you need it. I am grateful for your time, hope and energy.

Discrimination in the Civilian Workforce for being a Survivor

In 2016 Sep, I had sexual assault issues with one of my employers at a private security agency: I reported it to HR and was fired the next day "at will" state. That termination is also a discriminating factor when viewed in the eyes of the Law Enforcement Background check. (First job after discharge).

• In 2017 Jan, I was hired as a Federal Law Enforcement. I was there for a month and subsequently sexually assaulted in my home by SGT Eli. Once my work found out that I was assaulted they put me through two Internal Affairs investigations to "weed" me out. The Warden at the time said, "Because of what happened I don't deserve to be a law enforcement officer". I was being harassed and spread rumors by other law enforcement coworkers which prompted the second IA investigation. In the best interest of the department and my health at the time I resigned, and they lied and said, "I resigned due to accepting a position in another state ". (Second Job after discharge).

• In 2018 June, I was accepted to the Wisconsin State Law Enforcement Academy because I self-sponsored myself using the GI Bill - The students found out I was a SA survivor from the Military, so they outcast me, spread rumors, and exiled me from class. I told the Academy Director and he allowed me to restart the Academy in an alternate class. But rumors spread and so I was given a "contract" I had to follow with rules just for me. If I violated those unrealistic rules I would be exiled from the Academy. Rumors continue to spread that and one of the rules said I am not allowed to communicate with the rest of recruits. I was subsequently removed from the Academy but could go to a different Black Hawk Technical College. At that time, I completed 2018 June to 2018 October approximately 4 or 5 months of the academy.

• In 2019 to 2020, I worked for the local Emerald Queen Casino and faced sexual harassment twice. The second time I reported it in June 2020, my employer took me off duty and placed me on a 6 month "investigation" paid leave. I sought legal advice and talked to the Attorney General's Office in WA. I returned to work for 5 days. I was then transferred to another site where all three of my offenders were. It became a hostile work environment as a form of retaliation. That company wanted to suspend me for "violating a policy" by reaching out to my supervisor to tell him I cannot work with my offenders. I quit.

I soon learned that trying to work on my military injuries and simultaneously work would be challenging. Some days I would feel shameful or guilty for being a young woman and unable to consistently work normal civilian jobs. I soon learned I had a niche to speak and began making short form videos on my traumas to help others. It’s not a conventional job but it is peaceful and rewarding to know I am making a positive impact in other people’s lives.

COMMONLY ASKED MST QUESTIONS

What Is MST?

MST includes any sexual activity during military service where a Veteran was involved against their will. They may have been:

- Pressured into sexual activities (for example, with threats of negative consequences for refusing to be sexually cooperative or with implied better treatment in exchange for sex)
- Unable to consent to sexual activities (for example, when intoxicated or asleep)
- Physically forced into sexual activities

Other experiences that fall into the category of MST include:

- Unwanted sexual touching or grabbing, including during "hazing" experiences.
- Offensive remarks about a person's body or sexual activities that they found threatening.
- Unwelcome sexual advances that a person found threatening.

The identity or characteristics of the perpetrator, whether a Veteran was on or off duty at the time, and whether they were on or off base at the time do not matter.

How Common Is MST?

According to the Veterans Affairs (VA) national screening program, in which every Veteran seen for health care is asked whether they experienced MST, provides data on how common MST is among Veterans seen in VA. National data from this program reveal that about 1 in 3 women and 1 in 50 men respond "yes," that they experienced MST, when screened by their VA provider. Although rates of MST are higher among women, because there are many more men than women in the military, there are actually significant numbers of women and men seen in VA who have experienced MST. In fact, over 1 of every 3 Veterans who tell a provider they experienced MST are men.

It is important to keep in mind that these data speak only to the rate of MST among Veterans who have chosen to seek VA health care; they cannot be used to make an estimate of the actual rates of sexual assault and harassment experiences among all individuals serving in the U.S. Military.

How Can MST Affect Veterans?

Like other forms of trauma, MST can be a life-changing event. However, people are often remarkably resilient after experiencing MST. MST is an experience, not a diagnosis or a mental health condition, and there are a variety of reactions that Veterans can have in response to MST. Many individuals recover without professional help. Others may generally function well in their lives but continue to experience some level of difficulties or have strong reactions in certain situations. For some Veterans, the experience of MST may continue to affect their mental and physical health in significant ways, even many years later. The type, severity and duration of a Veteran's difficulties will vary based on factors like:

- Whether they have experienced other traumatic events
- Whether the MST happened once or was repeated over time
- The types of responses they received from others at the time of the MST

Gender, race/ethnicity, religion, sexual orientation and other cultural variables can also affect the impact of MST. Although every Veteran's reaction following MST is unique, many Veterans may struggle with similar issues. Some of the experiences many survivors of MST may have at some point include:

- **Strong emotions**: having intense, sudden emotional responses to things; feeling angry or irritable all the time; feeling depressed
- **Feelings of numbness**: feeling emotionally "flat"; difficulty experiencing emotions like love or happiness
- **Trouble sleeping**: trouble falling or staying asleep; disturbing nightmares
- **Difficulties with attention, concentration, and memory**: trouble staying focused; frequently finding their mind wandering; having a hard time remembering things
- **Problems with alcohol or other drugs**: drinking to excess or using drugs daily; getting intoxicated or "high" to cope with memories or emotional reactions; drinking to fall asleep
- **Difficulty with things that remind them of their experiences of sexual trauma**: feeling on edge or

"jumpy" all the time; difficulty feeling safe; going out of their way to avoid reminders of their experiences

- **Difficulties with relationships**: feeling isolated or disconnected from others; difficulty trusting others; trouble with employers or authority figures; abusive relationships; difficulties with intimacy or sex
- **Physical health problems**: chronic pain; weight or eating problems; gastrointestinal problems

Posttraumatic stress disorder (PTSD) is one of the most common mental health diagnoses among MST survivors. Other mental health diagnoses that are frequently related to MST include depression and other mood disorders and substance use disorders. MST has also been found to be associated with a variety of physical health conditions.
Fortunately, people can recover from experiences of trauma, and VA has effective services to help Veterans do this.
What MST-Related Services Does VA Offer?
VA is strongly committed to ensuring that Veterans have access to the help they need in order to recover from MST.

- Every VA health care facility has a designated **MST Coordinator** who serves as a contact person for MST-related issues. This person can help Veterans find and access VA services and programs.
- Recognizing that many survivors of sexual trauma do not disclose their experiences unless asked directly, VA health care providers ask every Veteran whether they experienced MST. This is an important way of making sure Veterans know about the services available to them.
- All treatment for physical and mental health conditions related to experiences of MST is provided **free of charge**.
- Veterans do **not** need to be service connected (or

have a VA disability rating). Veterans do **not** need to have reported the incident(s) at the time or have other documentation that they occurred to get care.

- Veterans may be able to receive this care even if they are not eligible for other VA care.
- MST-related services are available at every VA medical center and many VA community-based outpatient clinics.
- MST-related outpatient counseling is also available through VA's community-based Vet Centers.
- MST-related services are designed to meet Veterans where they are at in their recovery, whether that is focusing on strategies for coping with challenging emotions and memories or, for Veterans who are ready, discussing the impacts of their MST experiences in more detail with a trusted provider. Veterans can ask to meet with a clinician of a particular gender if it would help them feel more comfortable.
- For Veterans needing more intensive treatment and support, VA also provides MST-related mental health treatment in residential or inpatient settings.

For self-care, you can also download Beyond MST, a free mobile app that was created for survivors of MST to cope with MST-related challenges and improve health, relationships and quality of life.
Visit VA's MST website to learn more about VA's MST-related services.
How Can Veterans Get Help?
For more information, Veterans can:

- Speak with their existing VA health care provider.
- Contact the MST Coordinator at their nearest VA Medical Center.
- Contact their local Vet Center.
- Contact the Veteran's Crisis Line if they are in a crisis or need immediate assistance. Call 988 and press 1, or visit www.veteranscrisisline.net to reach caring, qualified responders trained to help Veterans. Many of them are Veterans themselves.

Although this page refers to Veterans, most former Service members with an Other Than Honorable or uncharacterized (entry-level) discharge can also receive MST-related care. Former National Guard and Reserves members with federal active duty service or a service-connected disability who were discharged under honorable conditions or with an Other Than Honorable discharge are also eligible; the service-connected disability does not need to be related to your experiences of MST. Current Service members can receive services related to MST, although for some types of services, a Department of Defense referral may be required. For more information, contact your local VA medical center and ask to speak with the MST Coordinator.

What are signs that I need help?

No two experiences are the same, and no two people will react the same way to a sexual assault. You may need help if you're facing the following:

- Being unable to enjoy intimacy
- Being unable to feel happiness or love
- Drinking excessively or using drugs
- Feeling disconnected from loved ones
- Feeling like hurting yourself
- Feeling numb
- Feeling on edge or unsafe
- Getting angry and irritable easily
- Getting involved in abusive relationships
- Having difficulty concentrating
- Having trouble sleeping and nightmares
- Struggling to remember things.
- Suffering with physical health problems, including chronic pain, sexual issues and stomach and bowel problems

Research has found that **negative social reactions to sexual assault disclosure** (e.g., blaming the victim, treating the victim differently, attempting to control the victim's actions, or focusing on one's own feelings rather than the victim's) are related to depression, substance abuse, and more severe PTSD symptoms among survivors. 4 – 6 On the other hand, positive social reactions (e.g., providing emotional support, offering resources, and explaining that it wasn't the victim's fault) are related to survivors having a greater perceived control over recovery, which is related to fewer PTSD symptoms.

How does MST impact our life?

Some of the most common difficulties following MST are posttraumatic stress disorder, depression, and problems with alcohol or substance use. Because of these symptoms, you may have difficulty functioning at work, school, or with other responsibilities. It can also be hard to maintain healthy close relationships.

Tips for sharing your story.

Sharing a sexual assault story can be an incredibly difficult and vulnerable experience. It is important to remember that every survivor's experience is unique, and there is no one "right" way to respond. However, here are some common responses that survivors have reported finding helpful:

1. **Believing the survivor**: Sexual assault is a traumatic experience, and it can be difficult for survivors to come forward. Believing them and validating their experience can be incredibly powerful.
2. **Offering support:** Survivors may need emotional support, practical help, or both. Ask them what they need and how you can help.
3. **Respecting their boundaries:** Survivors may need space or time to process their experience. Respect their boundaries and let them know that you are there for them when they are ready.
4. **Encouraging them to seek professional help:** Sexual assault can

have long-lasting effects on mental health. Encourage survivors to seek professional help if they feel comfortable doing so.

It is important to note that every survivor's experience is different, and what works for one person may not work for another. The most important thing is to listen to the survivor, believe them, and support them in whatever way they need.

Who is Vanessa Now? What happened to her?

Today is December 7, 2023. Three years have passed since this original book was written. Shortly after I wrote this book in October 2020, I lost my job due to covid and asking to seek medical treatment.

All my life I have felt different and like I never fit in with society. December 2020 to June 2023 I was chronically homeless. Finally, I am so grateful to have housing using the HUD VASH Veteran Section 8 voucher.

I relocated to Philadelphia, PA in May of 2022 to reunite with my daughter who had relocated to New Jersey on behalf of her father's military service. Attempted to work a few part time jobs. That took me down the yearlong path of being in an extremely physically abusive relationship while I waited for my voucher to be ready. In those 11 long months I was in a female veteran homeless shelter to and two toxic homes and now my apartment all to be closer to my daughter.

In the last few years, I have been creating content on social media as a public speaker for Mental Health and Military related Trauma. I have garnered over 100k followers on Tik Tok and still building over a 10k follower count on Instagram. I've been featured in several articles, news stations, speaking engagements and podcasts to share my story.

Feel free to follow me or Direct Message me if you have feedback or questions.

@UnseenUnheardSoldier
on Tik Tok/Instagram/X

One of my grandfather's dying wishes was that I share his story when I have a little more notoriety. My goal is to make a positive impact by public speaking all over the world and feeling daily gratitude for life. Thank you, Grandfather and Ancestors, for guiding me and allowing my manifestations actualize step by step.

FINAL THOUGHTS

I know sorry will never change anyone's life hardships but if any of you had to go through this and or maybe dealing with these issues now in the Military or post-service. I just want to tell you. You can heal. I am so proud of you. You chose to pick up this book. This book was made to also help validate other survivors who are not ready to speak yet.

To those still in the Military and going through these issues. I would recommend reporting restricted only unless you feel you have enough evidence. That way you can get help without your chain of command finding out. Another resource I did not know about was the Vet Center. You can go there, and they have Military Sexual Trauma professionals, and you can seek help while on Active Duty. Good references would be to watch the documentary "***The Invisible War***" to give you a good visual and testimonial insight on the Military processes. I would not want others to face retaliation and discharge the same way I did.

To male and female veterans who went through this before me, your sacrifices and your trauma is valid. I believe you. We believe you. I know all too well the impact this has on our psyche. If I can survive these challenges that I have faced. So, can you. Thanks for giving me a platform and for reading my story thus far. It may not be complete, but it gives you a good idea into the life of a Military Sexual Trauma Survivor. In the end we are all here for each other. We all bleed red. We all are human and have emotions. No human life is exempt from stress or life challenges but with education and knowledge we can learn to lessen it.

Being raped in the Military or civilian comes with a lot of trials and tribulations. But not everyone develops PTSD (Post Traumatic Stress Disorder) from it. You must recognize in yourself the symptoms and changes in your mind and body if you feel you need psychotherapy or treatment. It is okay to get help. As a survivor, an advocate, a fellow human being, a female, a minority, a Military disabled veteran and as a prior Federal Law Enforcement officer:

I implore you to keep going. There comes a time when you must want to take care of yourself. I am tired of being discriminated against for being a victim of a crime that I had no control over. Up until December 1, 2020 I did not believe in the phrase that "time can heal wounds". I will never stop being a human, a Soldier, a prior Law Enforcement Officer (Corrections and Police). Those skills are engrained in my body, my mind, my heart and my soul. I will continue to pursue my career as a humble, passionate, compassionate, active listening, and truth-seeking as an advocate and public speaker.

I know I can make a difference in my daily interactions with the citizens in my community that I serve. I am an amazingly effective communicator. I take the time to listen to every individual who crosses paths with me and blessed to make an acquaintance. If there is anything, that you take away from personal testimony. I say this with tears in my eyes. Take this message: ***The human body, brain and psyche can be repaired over time. Medication is your choice. I have done every form of therapy the Veteran Affairs has to offer, but they do not have my need of EMDR. I utilize coping skills every day. Where***

you might be debilitated with Post-Traumatic Stress syndrome now if you talk about it or write it down. Even share your own story. There is a theory called Post-Traumatic Growth. Please take away the amount of unbearable strength that I possess. The unmatchable resiliency. The courage to continue to live and serve, and undeniably tell this horrendous story. The previous pages will have images from the investigations, quotes, and other images. Stay hopeful. Tomorrow is a new day. Every day you are reborn to make new decisions, new thinking patterns.

Healing in life is not linear. There will be ups and downs. But you must seek help when you are ready to get help. It took me to die to appreciate a second chance in life.

Not everyone experiences near death experiences or woke up today. Taking care of your mental health is the number 1 priority. We cannot gain stability or focus on our health when we can't even function.

Do not take life for granted. Know that this experience happened to you, but we cannot allow it to consume or define us. I have been to the afterlife and returned. I deliberately chose to place my daughter in custody so I can take care of health physically and mentally/emotionally. That was a tough decision.

I believe I you. I care. Being raped, assaulted, verbally talked down too that was NEVER our faults. Fortunately, if you are reading this book then we have another day to heal and love ourselves despite our circumstance. Thank you to all who had interest in reading this book. Take what resonates and leave the rest.

RESOURCES

National Sexual Assault Hotline: a service of RAINN. Online chat hotline. Spanish online chat hotline. Telephone hotline: 800-656-HOPE (4673)

National Helpline for Male Survivors: a service of 1in6. Online chat hotline.

National Street Harassment Hotline: a service of Stop Street Harassment. Online chat hotline.

Safe Helpline - DOD Department of Defense Helpline
Call 877-995-5247 to relate to a trained, confidential.

Safe Helpline staff member, 24/7.
Veterans Crisis Line - for Veterans, Active-Duty Service Members 1-800-273-8255 press 1 or dial 988 on your phone.

National Domestic Violence telephone hotline: 800.799.SAFE

Down below are pictures of my family and military time.

Grandpa PFC Ronald A. Morbeck/ US ARMY and My Father

Grandpa PFC Ronald A. Morbeck/ US ARMY/ Yakima, WA

Grandpa PFC Ronald A. Morbeck/ US ARMY/ Date of Birth: May 21, 1939 to October 17, 2023

Private (E-2) Vanessa M. Morbeck/ US ARMY/ Fort Jackson, SC April 2012

Private First Class (E-3) Vanessa M. Morbeck/ US ARMY/ Camp Casey, South Korea September 13, 2012 to September 2013

Vanessa and her 8 year old daughter in Frankford Veterans Village in November 2023

If you have any questions, concerns, or want to reach out feel free to reach me.

With Love,

VANESSA MORBECK

Made in the USA
Columbia, SC
06 February 2025

53397780R00067